The Starrigans of
Little Brook Bottom

The Starrigans of Little Brook Bottom

by Harold Davis
Illustrated by Dana Carter

Tuckamore Books
a Creative Publishers imprint

St. John's, Newfoundland and Labrador
2005

Canada Council   Conseil des Arts
for the Arts   du Canada

We acknowledge the support of The Canada Council for the Arts for our publishing program.

We acknowledge the financial support of the Government of Canada through the Book Publishing Industry Development Program (BPIDP) for our publishing program.

Printed on acid-free paper

Published by
TUCKAMORE BOOKS
an imprint of CREATIVE BOOK PUBLISHING
a Transcontinental associated company
P.O. Box 8660, St. John's, Newfoundland and Labrador A1B 3T7

Printed in Canada by:
TRANSCONTINENTAL INC.

Library and Archives Canada Cataloguing in Publication

Davis, Harold, 1958-
     The Starrigans of Little Brook Bottom / by Harold
Davis; illustrated by Dana Carter.

ISBN 1-894294-85-8

     I. Carter, Dana, 1974-   II. Title.

PS8607.A86S7 2005   jC813'.6   C2005-902205-1

May this little tale give strength to the hope
that missing children everywhere
find their way safely home.

HD
Salmonier
March, 2005

Author's Note

This story is the product of my imagination, but it has been touched by many.

It never occurred to me, during that winter long ago when I was hauling logs around Little Brook Bottom, that I was having a literary experience. Joe Linehan, Sandy Wall, Bud Linehan and Ferg Tremblett shared the work, the frost, and the enormous suppers of that winter with me. Joe and Ferg are gone now. Ferg passed away before I wrote this, but Joe was able to read the manuscript in the weeks before he died.

Chapter One - An Encounter

A hundred years ago, on a big island in a cold ocean, an ancient river ran out of the forest and through the middle of a tiny settlement. The place was called Pinchgut, probably because of the prosperity of its first settlers.

On a hot afternoon in mid-summer the river sparkled in the sunshine, deceiving anybody looking across it into forgetting the deep winter freeze-ups and cold floods of spring. On the riverbank, at the edge of a meadow, a massive spruce tree leaned out over the river. It tilted so far that it made no sense for it to be there at all and you would expect, if you waited for just a few more minutes, to see it tumble into the river below. But it didn't fall. It hung there for more summers than anybody could remember, and through winters that nobody could forget.

Krab could see just about all of Pinchgut from his vantage point high up in the gnarly old tree. He was comfortable on his perch, up beyond where children picked the franklin from the tree-trunk, using it like their children would one day use chewing gum, up where the limbs were thick for lying on. It was a perfect place to see everything while remaining unseen himself—unseen by people. Krab knew the chickadees and robins could see him when they flew over the tree. The horses, cows, and sheep could see him, if they were inclined to walk to where he was, but the sun was hot and they chose not to move. A young weasel eyed him earlier as he moved along the riverbank. It had never met anything like Krab before, and hesitated to determine if he was a potential meal. A sharp warning set the weasel straight and it moved on. Krab understood its bewilderment. Many creatures never quite knew what to make of him. A human, if one chanced upon him, and depending on just where in the world the meeting occurred, would have called him a leprechaun, an elf, or most likely, a fairy. Krab, you see, was one of the little people—he was a starrigan.

He stretched out to his full length on the spruce bough. Anything giving the limb and its occupant a cursory glance could be forgiven for taking Krab for a young kitten. His body, except for his face, was covered with coarse brown hair that grew thicker around his middle, giving him a pot-bellied profile. His legs seemed too short for his chunky body while his head appeared to be a great deal too large. The feature most likely to be noticed by those seeing him for the first time would be his huge brown eyes. They were the eyes of a creature that saw much and learned from what they saw. The starrigans' eyes suited them well.

Down through the centuries starrigans had always taken care not to be seen by humans, but, in spite of their wariness, they were not always successful. Once Krab himself was careless. It happened during a howling storm three winters earlier.

The blizzard made it just about impossible to see the man standing by the log pile. He was dressed for the weather. His outer garments were oilskins—the jacket and pants were made from tough cotton canvas and treated with linseed oil to shed rain and snow with equal disdain. He wore home-knit woolen socks inside of leather boots also waterproofed by repeated applications of oil. Long woolen mitts, that had a forefinger as well as a thumb, protected his hands. Gunner's mitts they were called, but they were also favoured by loggers, who appreciated the dexterity they offered while working with clumsy logs and sharp axes. His head was covered with a wool cap that, like the rest of his garb, well suited the day, the occupation, and the man.

Michael heard the jingle of harness bells on the wind long before he could see the grey draft horse. Eventually, like a phantom fashioned from the blowing snow, the horse came out of the storm. It pulled a set of enormous wooden sleds. Two men sat on the front slide. The driver called out over the wind to the man waiting by the logs.

"Hello, young Duggan. Is that pile ready to go?"

"Ready when you are, Phil," the young man said. "Jim came along and scaled them a few minutes ago."

"Whoa there, Nell. Whoa now." Steam rose from the horse as the sleds stopped at the log pile.

"You cut all these today, Michael?"

"I'm good, Phil," Michael said, "but not that good. I started this lot yesterday evening. I'll help you load them."

"No need for that. Vince and I will do it. You keep on cutting."

"I'm done with cutting today," Michael said. "I'm heading home. I'm going to catch a ride out to the river with you fellows."

"Home, in the middle of the week?" Vince asked. "You must have your money made—or is it love? What do you think, Phil?"

"There's not enough money in the world to make me walk five miles in this mess," Phil said. "It must be love. Young fellow, are you feeling all right in the head?"

"You two can laugh if you like," Michael said, "but I promised Jenny that I'd be home today and if I don't show up, she'll probably send someone after me."

"She's about due to have her baby, isn't she?" asked Phil.

"She might've had it by now," Michael said. "When I left to come in here on Sunday, she looked like she was ready to burst."

The three of them piled the logs on the sleds. Vince tied a rope around the load and Michael and Phil used a stick to twist it tight. Satisfied that the logs were secure, all three of them climbed on and got comfortable. Phil whistled and slapped the reins. Nell leaned into her harness and, with little effort, started hauling the load along the path.

"As harsh as this weather is, I like working in it," Phil said. "It's not too cold."

"It's a lot easier cutting too," Michael said. "You only need to chop halfway through the tree and the wind takes it from there."

"It'll be a lot worse than this when you get up in the high country," Vince said. "You mind what you're doing up there. There're places where you won't be able to see the length of yourself."

"I'll be all right," Michael said. "There's still lots of daylight left."

"True enough," Phil said. "But take some tea and a bit of grub just in case you get in trouble. Have you got matches?"

"Can we stop at the camp for a minute? I'll grab some supplies."

"No problem," Phil said. "I'm stopping anyway to fill the stove with wood."

The three men sat on the logs with their backs to the wind, trying hard to keep the storm from penetrating their clothes. The world around them was white except for bits of dull green peeping out from under the snow plastered to the trees. Above the trees, enormous snow squalls crossed the sky to settle on the ridges. The wind and the snow on the ground muffled the sound of the horse's hoofs and harness bells, lulling the men into a trance that wasn't broken until they came to a small wooden bridge. Across the bridge, a cabin was tucked into the woods by the side of the brook. It was a humble affair with log walls, a rough board floor, and a roof of blackjack felt. The cabin blended so well into the surrounding woods, unless one knew its location, it could easily be overlooked. The horse, however, knew where it was and stopped in front of the door.

"I'll give Nell a drink while you fellows are inside," Vince said.

"Good idea," Phil said. "We'll only be a minute." He followed Michael inside the cabin. "It's all right that we did stop. The fire is just about out." He filled the half-drum stove with birch junks while Michael poked through the grub box.

"I got tea and sugar, bread, a bit of cheese, matches and dry socks," Michael said. He sat on a wooden bunk and tossed it all into his knapsack. "That's enough. I'm ready."

"You are?" Phil asked. "No axe, no kettle, no mug?"

"The axe I was using in the woods is already on the sled." He put the knapsack on his back. "I keep a tin can in my lunch-bag that I use for a kettle and a mug. Like I said, I'm ready."

Phil laughed as he took one last look around the camp before following Michael outside.

"How old are you, Michael?" Phil asked.

"Nineteen. Why?"

"No particular reason. I'm just laughing at how eager you are to get home. I wish I was nineteen again."

Water was still dripping from the horse's muzzle as the three woodsmen climbed on the sleds again. Phil slapped the reins and once more they were on their way. Ten minutes later they reached the river where thousands of logs were piled on the bank. The logs would stay there until spring floods came and it was time for the drive: the annual ritual of floating the logs down the river to the sawmill in Pinchgut. The three men jumped to the ground.

"Thanks for the ride," Michael said. "I'll give you a hand to unload."

"You get on your way," Phil said. "You got a long walk ahead of you. Me and Vince got the rest of the day to get this done."

"You sure?" Michael asked. "I don't mind helping."

"Get going, before we change our minds," Vince said. "And remember what I told you—be careful on the trail and don't do anything foolish."

"Stop worrying," Michael said. "I'll be all right."

He was halfway across the ice-covered river when Phil called to him. "Michael, be sure to tell Jenny we're thinking about her. Tell her I'll remember her tonight in my prayers."

Michael grinned, "Thanks, I'll tell her."

With that, he set out again. He enjoyed his hike, in spite of the blizzard. Most of his days were a grind of hard labour that left little time for thinking. A new wife and a baby on the way gave him plenty to think about. Jenny was beautiful. She could have had her pick of any of the young men who ever met her. He was still amazed and grateful that she chose him over all the others, but now he worried about her. Women sometimes died having babies. He wanted to get home to see that everything was all right.

His six-foot frame moved quickly and quietly as he worked his way through the stunted spruce growing in a boggy bottom. Now the path climbed up to a dry ridge where the trees were large and spaced far enough apart to allow for easy movement. As he walked in and out among the towering fir and birch, a sudden movement caught his eye. He looked up, expecting to see a bird or a rabbit. Then he cried out in alarm.

What looked to be a miniature man was somersaulting through the air. It landed, feet first, in a snowdrift that the wind was constructing by the side of the path. The apparition heard Michael's cry and turned towards him just long enough for each of them to stare into the eyes of the other; then the small one was gone. Michael felt a chill move through his body. His legs shook, and he dropped to his knees.

"Lord, help me," he said. "That was a fairy."

Michael stayed on his knees, praying, and waiting for whatever fate was to befall him. His mind and soul told him to expect horrors beyond imagination. Since he was a child he heard stories about the fairies. He remembered making himself as small as he could in the corner of his grandparents' kitchen, too frightened to move, while the old people whispered about the fairies' magic. They told tales about the mischief the mystical ones caused, and how they led people away, never to be heard from again. Michael expected he was about to find out all about the fairies' evil.

Meanwhile, just above Michael's head, in a hole that had been occupied by a family of woodpeckers a few months earlier, Krab lay panting and cursing his own stupidity.

"He saw me! Heaven help me, he saw me. I have to get away or I'm done for." His whole body was shaking. He too had heard tales, but they told about people capturing his kind and keeping them in a cage. "I'll never see Little Brook Bottom again."

Michael, still on his knees, in the middle of a blizzard, in the middle of the woods, in the middle of the winter, began to sort through the myths in his mind. Nothing had happened since his encounter. Whatever it was that he saw—and Michael never doubted for an instant that he had seen something—didn't really look all that dangerous. In fact, the more he thought about it, he couldn't help but conclude that the fairy, if that's what it was, looked like it was having fun jumping in the snow. Slowly, he got to his feet and looked around. He saw nothing but trees and blowing snow—

exactly what Krab was praying for as he trembled in the tree just above the woodsman.

Michael stumbled to where an old tree lay on the ground and sat down on it. The victim of some long-ago gale, the blowdown lay sheltered from the snowstorm among the young evergreens. Some things were clear to Michael. He did see something and he was far from any help; yet it didn't hurt him.

"Maybe they're not as bad as they're made out to be," he thought. There was no reason to believe otherwise. He stared out across the barrens. The blowing snow looked like a white wall. He would have to figure this out later. He needed to get home to Jenny while it was still daylight. He picked up his axe and bag and leaned into the blizzard. But before he left the ridge, he took one last look back through the snow.

Still huddled inside the woodpecker's nest, Krab heard him speak.

"I don't know what you are, but I know you were here and probably still are." (Krab took little comfort from that.) "I don't mean you any harm. My wife is having a baby and, if you're something good, I'd appreciate anything you can do to keep them safe."

With that Michael turned toward home. He never looked back again for the two hours it took him to reach his own house. If he had, he may have made the trip somewhat faster.

Krab watched from his hiding place as Michael left the ridge and started out across the barrens. He kept his eyes on the young man until he could no longer see him in the swirling snow. Then, instead of escaping from the tree, Krab leaned back in the comfort of the round burrow and thought about what had happened. Minutes after he allowed himself to be seen, Krab expected the man to try to catch him. That's what humans did—according to everything that he had ever heard about them. This man, however, seemed to be just as frightened as Krab. The man certainly knew Krab was close by, even if he didn't know exactly where he was hiding. Krab pondered what he said, especially the part about keeping the mother and baby safe.

That puzzled the little starrigan. Through the ages his kind avoided contact with humans—and for good reason as far as he knew. Yet, this man asked for his help. One thing was certain: Krab had a burning need to know more, and the answer to his questions was getting farther away with every passing moment.

He leapt from the woodpecker's nest and landed more than twenty feet from the tree. A few more bounds took him out of the ridge and on to the barrens. He moved with the mystical speed that had well served his kind for centuries. From tree to ground to berry bush, and then back to the tops of the stunted trees of the barrens again, he moved faster than any animal of the ground or air. The speed of the little ones was the stuff that gave rise to legends among humans, for many of the chance encounters between them and starrigans had been so fleeting that the humans were left unsure if they had seen something or had been deceived by their eyes and minds.

In short order Krab had Michael in sight. He moved carefully, watching to make sure that the man didn't see him again, but he need not have worried. Michael was only looking for the fastest route to home. Soon the path brought them to the open expanse of a frozen pond where Michael stopped. He gazed across the pond and then looked to where the path turned to meander along the shoreline. Krab stopped and hid just a few feet from Michael's shoulder in the dense evergreen branches of some young firs. The young man gingerly stepped out on the ice and lifted his axe. He made two strong chops and then examined the hole in the ice. Satisfied the ice was safe to walk on, he started out across the pond. Krab faced a dilemma. There was absolutely nowhere to hide out on the ice. He would certainly be seen if the woodsman turned and looked. On the other hand, he wasn't sure where Michael was going, and if he took the long way around the pond he could lose him among the numerous paths on the other side. Krab made a decision that would have been unthinkable a short while earlier, but would cause his status among the starrigans to climb immeasurably in the days ahead.

He leapt from the tree and landed on Michael's knapsack.

Krab clung to the outside of the bag, ready to leap back to the trees if Michael gave any indication of being aware of his passenger. Fortunately for Krab, the howling wind and slippery ice underfoot demanded all of Michael's attention. On they went, into the teeth of the gale. Soon they reached the shoreline on the far side. Here the forest once again provided cover for Krab and he left his unsuspecting ride.

Michael didn't stop or slow down. On he pushed with Krab close on his heels. More than an hour later they broke out of the forest into a meadow at the mouth of the river. A tidy, two-story, peaked-roof house stood on the riverbank. Michael smiled when it came into sight. The house was a source of pride and joy for him. After Jenny accepted his marriage proposal they decided to have their wedding reception in their own house—they just had to build it first. That winter family and friends turned out to help Michael cut more than a thousand logs. He arranged to have the logs sawed 'on the halves' at the mill, so the lumber and framing cost nothing except hard work. They scrimped and saved to buy nails, window glass, and bricks for the chimney. The stove was a gift from his parents. Just about every able-bodied soul in the place helped with the construction, and the last coat of paint was dry just in time for the wedding supper. Today, however, the contentment he felt seeing his house didn't last.

He was uneasy about Jenny, and whatever it was he saw in the ridge only added to his restlessness. The weather was as bad as he had ever seen it and he was completely unsatisfied with his progress.

"At least Island Pond was frozen over and I didn't have to walk all the way around it," he said.

He made his way across the windswept meadow towards his house. He didn't expect anybody to be out on a day like this, and was surprised to see several men gathered where the porch and woodshed provided some shelter from the storm. A sudden, terrible dread chilled him to the bone. Something was wrong. Two of the men came towards him. In front was his father, Ned, followed closely by his older brother, Thomas. Michael dropped his axe and knapsack and ran to meet them. Krab listened from behind a fence post.

"What's wrong?" Michael asked.

"Michael, stop," his father said. "Listen to me." Ned Duggan grabbed his son's shoulders to stop him from going any further. He looked into his son's eyes and picked his words carefully. "Jenny went into labour yesterday. She's having a hard time."

"How bad is she?" Michael asked.

"Not good. Your mother and Lucy think the baby is turned the wrong way."

"Let me go. I've got to see her."

"Wait, there's more," Ned said. He blocked his son's move to go around him and tightened his grip on the young man's shoulders. "Lucy told us to get the priest. Edmund is gone for him now. They should soon be here."

"She needs the priest? You mean she's dying?" Michael asked. "Oh God, I'm going to be sick."

Ned couldn't have dealt his son a harder blow if he had struck him with a hammer. Summoning the priest was never done lightly, and was a sure sign of imminent death. Ned continued to speak, never loosening the iron grip that he had on his son.

"Settle down, Michael. You need to be strong for Jenny. If she sees you're afraid she might lose whatever fight she has left. Do you understand me?"

Michael nodded. "Maybe I shouldn't go in yet," he said. "I should wait until she's better. She might be having the baby now."

"You have to go in, Michael," his father said. "She's waiting for you. She knows you're coming home today."

He felt himself being released from his father's grip and stumbled towards the house. He did not say anything as he entered the small porch on the back of the house. Out of habit, he took off his boots and hung his coat and cap on a nail behind the door. He climbed the narrow stairs to the second floor. Jenny's eyes opened when she heard him come in the bedroom.

"Michael, is that you?" she asked quietly.

"It's me. I'm here."

His mother, Sues, and the midwife, Lucy O'Reilly, moved aside as Jenny reached for his hand. He knelt close to her pillow and put his head against hers. He stroked her hair and smiled at her.

"Michael, it's hard," she whispered. "I'm trying but the baby's not coming. I don't know what to do."

"Shush," Michael said. "Just hold on a little while longer. It's going to be all right."

He had barely stopped from crying out when he saw her. The ordeal had taken a terrible toll. Her hair was matted with sweat, and the exhaustion and strain of her labour showed on her face, but it was the fear in her eyes that stabbed Michael.

"The baby will be here soon and you'll be all right," he said. "I'm here with you now. I love you."

Jenny tried to smile and was about to say something when wracks of pain seized her body. Michael bolted upright, alarmed at the violence and intensity of his wife's agony. The women descended on her immediately, pushing Michael away from the bed and back against the wall.

"It's OK, my love," Lucy said. "Try to take deep breaths. That's it, breathe deep. The pain will stop soon."

But it didn't stop. Another wave followed the first, and then another one close after that. Jenny's eyes rolled back in her head and her whole body shook from the assault. Her breaths, when she could breathe at all, came in shallow gasps. Michael knew that no living creature could withstand such agony very long.

"Jenny—"

"Go out, Michael," Lucy said. "This is no place for a man."

The midwife herded him out through the bedroom door and then followed him into the hallway. Her expression said more than her words.

"This isn't good, Michael," Lucy said. "The baby hasn't moved since last night. I'm doing everything I can, but it isn't working." She took hold of both Michael's hands. "I'll keep trying, but I don't know how much longer she can go on."

"Isn't there something we can do?" Michael asked. "I can't just leave her suffering like that."

Lucy squeezed his hands harder. "Pray for her," she said. "I'll do whatever I can. Stay close by in case she wants you."

It was small comfort to Michael, but he knew his wife couldn't be in more capable care. Lucy and her husband Joe didn't have any children of their own, but she had delivered just about every child born in Pinchgut for the past fifty years. Michael knew that her concern for Jenny was as great as his own, but she couldn't work miracles—and it looked like Jenny needed a miracle now.

Ned and Thomas were still outside when Michael came out. More men, including Lucy's husband, Joe O'Reilly, had joined his father and brother. Joe, who was best known throughout Pinchgut as Old Joe, was a lean and leathery giant who stood well over six feet and was reputed to be made of iron. He was past eighty, yet could still hold his own when travelling through the woods with men half his age. He was a friend to everyone and a tower of strength in the face of adversity. He took a step towards Michael, but the young man held up a hand to stop him, and went straight to the wood-shed. Old Joe looked at Ned who just shook his head in response to the unspoken question. There was nothing that either of them could do to help, so it was just as well to allow Michael his solitude.

Inside the shed Michael stumbled to a big square juniper junk and sat down. Alone there in the cold, with only the pale semi-light of the winter evening coming through the shed's dust-caked window, he tried to come to grips with the unbearable.

Jenny was dying.

Cold, salty tears streamed down his face. His lips quivered. He prayed every prayer that he knew.

"This isn't fair. She's young and she's good. She can't die." He pounded his knees with his fists. "Please let her live. She's trying to have a baby."

No doubt Michael hoped his prayers were being heard in heaven and perhaps they were, but one creature did hear Michael. Krab was hiding on top of the wood and hadn't missed a thing since the young man arrived home. He left his hiding place behind the fence post while the men watched Michael go into the house. When they huddled together to talk about what was happening, and how Michael might cope, he scurried past them and made his way up a dogberry tree growing near the bedroom window. From the bare tree he leapt to the window ledge and observed what was going on.

Krab was as shocked as Michael at Jenny's agony. The starrigan understood the process of birth. It was as much a part of nature as flowers in the spring and the flowing of the river. The starrigans celebrated birth as the greatest of all the works of nature. Yet here, before his eyes, the great miracle had turned evil and was about to take away life. Krab didn't understand it, but everything that he knew told him this was wrong.

"Please, somebody, somewhere help us," Michael said. His face was soaked with tears. "Please don't let her die."

Krab had an overwhelming desire to help set things right, but knew it was no simple matter. The essence of all natural things, the process of birth and death, was amiss here. Much of it was beyond his ability to understand, and all of it was far beyond his ability to remedy. He needed the help of someone who possessed the wisdom of the ages, the oldest and wisest of his kind. He had to go to Savid.

Chapter Two - A Decision

Krab scooted out through a rat hole in the shed and was hidden immediately by the gusting snow. His movements were so swift that the sharpest eye would never see him, nor would any living creature be sure what had passed by them. Across the meadow and into the forest Krab went. Soon Island Pond was in front of him and, just as quickly, left behind. Across the frozen barrens and marshes the starrigan sped until he passed through the ridge where he had first encountered Michael. Down into the bottomlands he dashed, and then across the big river and along the riverbank until he came to Little Brook. He followed Little Brook upstream, past where the woodsmen were now sheltered in their cabin for the evening, until he came to a tiny path that led into a densely wooded knoll. There he stopped. He had reached the home of the starrigans in Little Brook Bottom.

Krab plunged into the path. It wound its way through what appeared, from the outside, to be an impenetrable tangle of stunted spruce trees, alders, and berry bushes woven so tightly that only hints of light penetrated. The lack of light along the labyrinth gave the illusion of entering a subterranean chamber. He rushed along, brushing past several other starrigans. They were surprised because the usually affable Krab didn't stop to talk, so they followed him to find out what was going on.

The path brought him into a clearing. Overhead, a web of saplings, shrubbery, and other vegetation provided a canopy for one side of the glade. The other side was open to the heavens allowing several trees, most notably a huge witch-hazel, to reach skyward. The hillside on the sheltered end was covered with the entrances to dozens of burrows. The starrigans lived in a wild and often harsh land, but this thicket provided shelter, comfort, and security for them, and it was here that more than a hundred of Krab's clan lived. He hurried to the centre of the community.

"Where's Savid?" he asked. "I need to talk to her right away."

"Krab, what is it?" asked a starrigan named Soc.

"You look like you saw a crunnock," said another called Gable.

Krab brushed them aside and hurried to where a smooth root formed a comfortable seat. It was one of old Savid's favourite resting places. Seeing she wasn't there he scurried to the burrow where she slept. Just about every starrigan in the clan was following him by now, all clamouring for him to stop and tell them what was going on.

"Savid," he said, "where are you? I need help." Krab bolted from crevice to corner with the mob of noisy starrigans close at his heels.

"What is going on here?" rasped a familiar voice.

Krab turned to see an ancient starrigan step out of a whorl hollowed in the trunk of the witchhazel tree. She was tiny, even for a starrigan. The stoop of old age made her look even smaller. The decades had bleached all colour from her coat leaving it completely silver. Every passing winter and every new summer carved more lines into her face. She secured each step with the assistance of a staff of twisted black spruce that she clutched with both gnarled hands. She claimed she could no longer hear some of the sounds of the

world, but often added in the same breath that much of the noise was no longer worth listening to anyway. Her eyes showed that, while she had decided not to participate in the excited frenzy that the others had worked themselves into, she had missed nothing. The bouncing and chattering starrigans knew, even though her body was old and worn, her mind held great stores of knowledge. Savid started towards him but, before she could take two steps, Krab landed in front of her.

"Savid, I need your help. There's not much time," he said.

"No time for what?" Savid said.

"I saw a man."

"A man? Where? Is he here?"

"No, no," Krab said. "Up in the woods. He saw me."

The starrigans let out a collective gasp. "Oh no, Krab. Are you hurt?"

"I'm OK," Krab said. "It's the man's wife and baby. Savid, you have to help them."

"The man's wife and baby are up in the woods?" Savid said. "In this blizzard?"

"No, the baby is not in the woods," Krab said. "It's not born yet."

Confusion grew among the raucous starrigans and questions came from all sides.

"Not born yet?"

"Did you hear that?"

"She's having a baby in the woods by herself."

"The poor woman. Savid can we help her?"

Finally Savid took Krab by the arm and turned away from the crowd. A quick disapproving glance over her shoulder held the starrigans at bay. She moved Krab several paces away. He started to speak, but Savid put her forefinger to her pursed lips.

"Shush," she said. "Start at the beginning, my love, and tell me everything." She turned her attention to the others for a second. They were all leaning forward in anticipation. "And whoever makes a squeak will be gathering nippers' eggs for the rest of the winter."

That quieted the uproar in a hurry. Every starrigan knew that nippers hide their eggs so well that finding them was next to impossible. On top of that, old Savid was very particular about the quality of the nippers' eggs that she would accept. Besides, they all wanted to hear what Krab was going to say.

Krab began his tale, starting with how he had first encountered Michael at the ridge. The starrigans hung on every word, clutching each other anxiously as he told about hiding in the woodpecker's nest, and then "ohhing" and "ahhing" in disbelief as he related travelling to the human's home. Even old Savid, who thought she had lived long past the point where she would ever hear anything new, had to stop Krab and get him to repeat the part about crossing Island Pond on Michael's back. Her intensity deepened, however, when Krab began to recount what was happening with Jenny and the baby. She made him explain in detail everything he had seen and heard, instructing him to make certain he did not leave anything out or add anything he wasn't sure about.

Soon Savid and the others understood both the crisis and the assistance that Krab was seeking on behalf of the young family. Many starrigans were almost moved to tears by the plight of the humans. They stared at Savid to see what her response would be.

"It is good that you want to help," Savid said, "but what you want to do is to interfere with the cycle of life itself. Life comes to all creatures, but so does death. It is the certainty of death that makes life so precious."

"But, Savid," Krab said, "young mothers and babies are supposed to live. All around us creatures have their young. The mothers don't die."

"You're right," Savid said. "Young mothers and their babies are supposed to get a chance at life, but for some reason nature has made things different this time. We should never try to change what nature has determined to be right."

"If it is meant for the mother and baby to die," Krab said, "then it will happen no matter what we do. But what if they were supposed to live and something just went wrong?"

"What do you mean?"

"I've heard you say many times that all things happen for a reason," Krab said.

"Go on."

"Why it is that today," Krab asked, "of all days, the man saw me and I followed him home? Why did he ask me to help his wife and baby?" Krab looked around at all the starrigans. "He didn't even know she was dying when he asked for help. I believe it all happened because they are not meant to die."

Savid pondered this theory. Krab's logic made her think that perhaps higher powers were at work. Still, she had grave doubts.

"Krab," she said, "have you thought about what could happen if the child and mother lived when they were not supposed to? A single life can change the face of the world. The risks are great."

"What if the child is meant to do good and doesn't get the chance?" Krab asked. "All we know is that, for some reason, we've been allowed to try and make a difference."

"I share your sympathy for Jenny and her baby, but humans have a dark side," Savid said. "One of them can bring misery to millions."

"They can also do a lot of good," Krab said.

"That's true. It's possible that powers we don't understand may be at work, but I have to depend on my own judgement." She walked back to her seat in the witchhazel tree and sat down. For several long minutes she did not say anything. Finally, she turned to Krab and said, "I do believe, as you point out, that all things happen for a reason. Strange things have happened today. I will try to help."

Krab breathed a sigh of relief. "Thank you."

"Only time will tell if we are doing the right thing," Savid said. "I must prepare what you need. It won't take long."

Savid retreated to her burrow. Inside, away from the eyes of the other starrigans, she took a small packet from a ledge. The problem before her was difficult and required one of her most powerful remedies. Outside, the other starrigans continued to question Krab.

"Aren't you afraid they might catch you if you go back?" Soc said.

"You're going to end up in a cage," Mot said. "You must be crazy." He was big for a starrigan, and not known for his patience.

"I'm careful, and I don't think they want to hurt us," Krab said.

"Not careful enough," Mot said. "They already saw you once."

"That was an accident. Besides, I have to help them or Jenny and the baby will die."

"You're a fool, Krab," Mot said. "You'll get yourself caught, or drag them back here."

Krab shook his head and turned away. A squabble with Mot was the last thing he needed right now. He just hoped he wouldn't be too late getting back to the little house by the river.

Time was running out for Jenny and her baby. She lapsed in and out of consciousness as waves of pain continued their assault. Michael had been inside the shed for less than a half-hour when he heard a horse and sleigh.

He heard Ned speak. "Thank you for coming, Father."

"I came as fast as I could, Ned. How is she?" Michael recognized Father Quigley's voice.

"Not good, Father," Ned said. "You go on inside. I'll get Michael."

The priest was already going into the house when Michael opened the shed door and stepped out. He met his father coming towards him. Ned looked at his son.

"Mike, I know it's hard, but there's still hope," he said. "We have to go in."

Michael said nothing as he followed his father inside. More of their neighbours had gathered in the kitchen. They murmured words of support to Michael. He took off his coat and boots and went upstairs.

"Is she asleep?" he asked his mother.

"She stays awake for a few minutes," Sues said, "but then she passes out. I wish she would stay asleep. She's not in pain then." She put her arms around her son.

"Does she know what's going on?" Michael asked.

"I think so," Sues said.

Father Quigley opened his prayer book. Michael trembled as the clergyman prepared to pray.

"I hope she stays asleep," Michael said to his mother. But it wasn't to be.

"Michael," Jenny gasped. "Michael."

"I'm right here," he said. "It's going to be OK." He knelt by the bedside so that his head touched hers.

"No, it's not," Jenny whispered. "I'm dying. I know it. The baby is, too."

"No, Jenny," Michael said, "you're not going to die. You'll soon have the baby."

She shook her head. He could see that she wanted to say more, but just speaking was requiring a great effort. He leaned close to her face.

"I'm scared, Michael. Please stay with me. Hold my hand until it's over."

He clasped Jenny's hand and put his head on the pillow beside her. "I love you. I'll be here as long as you want me."

"Michael,"

Father Quigley said, "I should anoint her now while she's awake."

Michael nodded. He knew what the priest meant: *while she's still alive.* He held Jenny's hand tightly as the priest began. Michael sobbed while the others responded to the prayers at the appropriate times. Soon the ritual was completed and the priest moved to Michael's side.

"Remember Michael, while there's life there's hope," Father Quigley said. "But it's not in our hands. Pray for her. She needs a miracle now." The priest could do nothing more for Jenny. Now he had to brace the young man to cope with the death of his wife and child. "Heaven, show me the way," he said to himself.

Savid came out of her burrow. She held a pouch made from the soft inside bark of a birch tree. Its edges were sealed on three sides with spruce resin, and the top flap was wrapped several times around the entire packet. She gave it to Krab.

"This is what you need," Savid said. "It will help her and the baby, but only if they are meant to live. Jenny must breathe it in."

"How can I get her to do that?" Krab asked. "There are people all around her."

"If it is meant to be then a way will present itself," Savid said. "If you can't give it to her, it was never meant that you should."

"I understand."

"Remember, Krab," Savid said, "she must breathe it in deeply or it won't work. Hurry now."

Out from the knoll and along the riverbank Krab sped. The little starrigan dashed across the river and through the bottoms. He raced through the forest until he was once again outside of Michael's and Jenny's house. Getting inside was no problem. Numerous people came and went, some bringing prayers and foodstuffs, others just trying to find out the news. He made it upstairs by ducking under the long black coat of someone named "Father" who had come down to get a drink of water.

Once inside the room he darted into the closet. He was alarmed to see that Jenny was much worse. Clearly, her time was all but gone. His task was more difficult now as well. There were now four women in the tiny room, plus Michael, and a couple of more men. They surrounded Jenny. Krab could see no way to get near her.

He remembered what Savid said. *If it is meant that we should help, a way will present itself.*

Krab tucked himself in the corner of the closet and waited to see what would happen. He didn't have to wait long. The porch door continued to be left open as people came and went. An ugly stray tomcat, that Jenny fed and Michael tolerated, eyed the open door. Being a creature on a perpetual quest for food, it went inside. The crowd in the kitchen paid it no heed. It watched other people going upstairs and followed them. The cat surveyed the scene inside the bedroom with little interest until its eyes came to the closet. It spotted Krab, and instinctively crouched to pounce on the prospective meal. Krab saw the cat as soon as it came into the room and was ready. He bared his teeth and twisted his face into a ferocious display that terrified the cat. It arched its back and hissed a loud warning.

"Get that thing out of here," Lucy said.

Father Quigley and Ned both reached for the cat. It leapt from the floor to the bed and then ran out through the bedroom door, bawling loudly as it ran. The commotion took everybody's attention away from Jenny. Krab saw his chance. He bounded from the closet to Jenny's face. Her eyes were closed but she moaned gently, feeling him there. In a second he dumped the contents of the packet on her nose and in her mouth and leapt back to his hiding place.

"Will it work?" he wondered.

Jenny gagged and began to cough. All attention returned to her.

"Are you all right?" Lucy asked. "Do you want some water?"

"Something is happening," she gasped. "The baby is moving. I can feel it. It's coming." She propped herself up on her elbows and gritted her teeth. The fear that was in her eyes earlier was gone. Everybody in the room stared at her and then at each other.

"Are you sure?" Lucy asked.

"Yes," Jenny said. "The pain is different. I'm going to have the baby."

"Lucy," Michael said, "is she going to be all right?"

"Please God she will," Lucy said. The midwife became a bundle of energy and took charge of the room again. "Sues, you stay with me. The rest of you, get downstairs."

They all obeyed and piled down the stairs.

"Come on, Mike, we'll wait outside," Ned said. He led his dazed son through the sweltering kitchen and into the storm that was still blustering outside.

"What happened?" Michael asked when they were outdoors. "Is she going to be all right?"

"It looks like we might be getting the miracle we prayed for," Ned said. "You're going to be a daddy!"

"Get used to changing diapers, Mike," Edmund said to his older brother. "Don't worry if you don't get it right the first time. You'll get lots of practice."

"Better buy a cow, young fellow. I have one that I might let you talk me into selling cheap," Old Joe said. He had seen too many untimely deaths during his long life, and was well pleased with the positive turn.

The optimism was contagious. Michael smiled for the first time since he got home.

"That's the spirit, brother," Thomas said. "Come in the shed. I'll make a fire and we'll wait it out together."

Inside the shed Thomas lit a kerosene lantern and expertly split some dry junks of wood into kindling. In minutes he had a fire roaring in the cut-off drum that served as a stove.

The warmth radiated quickly and the men doffed their heavy coats and caps. Pipes and pouches appeared, and before long the air was thick with tobacco smoke.

Upstairs in the bedroom Krab was still tucked away in the closet. When Lucy O'Reilly pushed the crowd out of the room she closed the door, cutting off his only exit. It didn't matter; the curious little starrigan had no intention of leaving. Jenny was working hard to bring her baby into the world.

"Good girl," Lucy said. "Your baby will be in your arms before you know it."

"You're doing wonderful," Sues said. "Do you feel okay?"

"Better than before," Jenny panted. "I just want to have my baby."

"Don't worry," Lucy said. "It won't be long now."

Sues looked at Lucy. "I can't get over the change," she said. "Did you ever witness anything like it before?"

"No, my dear," Lucy said. "That was the biggest turn-around I ever saw in my life."

"How much longer?" Jenny asked between labour pains.

"This is your first baby," Lucy said. "It's going to be a while yet, my love."

They continued to encourage her as the labour continued, all they could do now was make Jenny as comfortable as possible and wait for the baby's arrival. In the shed the men were discussing the strange turn of events. No longer able to tolerate the heat in the kitchen, Father Quigley joined them. He was unwilling to leave before what he was sure was a miracle had finally played out.

"I never saw anything like it in all my days," Ned said. "One minute she was just about gone and then, all of a sudden, she came right out of it."

"She told me she was dying. She asked me to hold her hand until it was over," Michael said. "Father Quigley even anointed her. Then, she started to cough and said she felt the baby moving."

"You'll get the credit for this one, Father," Thomas said. "I'd say if the bishop hears about it, you'll be up for a promotion."

"Thank you, Thomas," the priest said, "but I don't want any promotions or any credit for what's happening. I can only offer prayers. A higher power than me delivers the miracles, and this is one for sure."

"Amen to that," Ned said.

"Did you think she was dying?" Michael asked the priest.

"I've watched a lot of people die over the years," Father Quigley said. "Some fooled me and got better, but I've never seen anybody that far gone come back. Jenny wasn't meant to die tonight, my son."

"Did she get better as soon as you anointed her?" Edmund asked Father Quigley.

"It was a while after that, I believe," the priest said. "It was when that tomcat came in the room, wasn't it, Ned?"

"That's right, Father," Ned said. "Remember the racket it made. I never saw a cat go nuts like that before."

"Maybe he saw something you didn't," Thomas said.

The priest, Ned, and Michael all looked at each other. None of them cared to contradict him.

Ned decided to get Michael's mind away from the stress for a while. "How are you making out with the logs?"

"The best kind," Michael said. "I'd say that everybody is knocking down at least fifty a day. Nice ones too— all twelve and fourteen feet long."

"Where are you fellows cutting this year?" Father Quigley said.

"Little Brook Bottom," Michael said. "There are plenty of nice ridges in there. We should be good for five or six winters."

"Are Phil and Vince having any problems getting the logs hauled to the river?" Thomas asked.

"They're hauling them as fast as we cut them," Michael said. "The paths are perfect. I'd say we have more than ten thousand piled now."

"Sounds like you're all working hard," Old Joe said. "You must have a good cook."

"The best," Michael said. "We never have the same thing twice in a row. It's boiled beans one day, baked beans the next. After that it could be stewed beans or cold beans—pea soup on Fridays."

"Ah, you fellows have it easy," Old Joe said. "The good life is making you soft."

"Really, Joe," Father Quigley said, "I didn't think anything could make life in the woods soft."

"Well, Father, it depends on how you look at it," Joe said. "As far as I'm concerned living is easier now than it ever was."

"What's so different from when you were my age?" Michael asked. A chorus of groans erupted from the others.

"Sit back everybody," Ned said. "We're going to hear a story now." Old Joe laughed with the rest of them before he started to speak.

"I'll try not to bore you," he said. "The big difference, Michael, is people. There were only three houses here when I was a boy." He rooted around in his pockets for his tobacco pouch and pipe. "This was only a place to stop and boil the kettle when you were going somewhere else. Now there are people to lend a hand whenever it's needed."

"That's true enough," Michael said. He looked around the shed at his friends. "I'm happy enough because you fellows are here with me today."

"Well, thank you, young Michael," Old Joe said. "I'm sure I speak for everyone here when I say that we appreciated the opportunity."

The men laughed while Michael just shook his head.

"I'm not saying another word, Mr. O'Reilly," Michael said. "You have the floor."

Old Joe laughed and then stood up and went to the stove. He poked through the burning junks to find a glowing brand to light his pipe. Once he had the pipe working to his satisfaction he sat down again and stared at the flames flickering through the cracks in the stove.

"Nobody has to face trouble alone anymore," he said. "Times like this, I look back at how it was when I was the age of young Michael there." He pointed at Michael with the stem of his pipe. "It came down to this. We had three choices: scratch for yourself, leave, or die. Just trying to make sure there was something more than elbows on the supper table, meant you had to be able to grow it or kill it."

"We still do lots of that," Ned said.

"True enough," Old Joe said, "but there's no danger of starvation now. There's work at the mill and we can always buy something to eat—even if it is a bit on the rough side and don't make us fat."

"Did you really risk starvation, Joe?" Father Quigley asked.

"I was lucky, Father," Old Joe said. "I always had my health and strength and managed to stay a step ahead of it, but there were lots of times when I brought a few rabbits or a couple of ducks to people who didn't have a tooth-full of their own left to eat."

"It's hard to believe things were that bad," Father Quigley said.

"Father," Old Joe said, "I've seen good people close to freezing to death because they had no wood and didn't have the strength to cut any. Imagine, living here in the middle of the woods and not able to get anything to burn for the want of something to eat."

"There was no choice but to help each other," Ned said. "You never knew when you might be the one needing help next. All it took was sickness or a broken leg to put you at the mercy of God."

"That's right," Old Joe said. "The only thing that I can ever remember being afraid of in my life was not being able to provide for myself." He took a long draw from his pipe. "Let me tell you, I hope those days are never heard tell of again, but it'd be a mistake for you young fellows to even think that they can't come back. They can—in a heartbeat."

As the night wore on the stories continued. Father Quigley regaled them with a hilarious yarn about how he decided, as a young priest, to hire a housekeeper to save himself from starving to death. Never one to be outdone, Old Joe followed with an outlandish tale about catching a beaver so far in the woods that he couldn't carry it home, so he cobbled together a leash and walked it out. By the time they got to Pinchgut, they were such good buddies that he didn't have the

34

heart to kill it and had to hike it back to its home a few days later.

The hours dragged on, but the men stayed with Michael. He knew they would. In the middle of the night he raided the kitchen pantry and brought out bread, butter, and two bottles of preserved bakeapple jam. Thomas brewed tea for all of them and they toasted the bread on the wood stove. The conversation died down. A few of the men dozed. Michael didn't sleep but a tremendous weariness had settled on him. He just noticed that the blizzard had blown its course, allowing him to see the sun rising over the eastern woods, when he was startled by his mother calling out to him from the porch door.

"Michael, come in right away. Hurry."

He didn't need to be called twice. He raced into the house and up the stairs. He was stopped at the open bedroom door by the most miraculous sight he ever laid eyes on.

Jenny was smiling at him from the bed, and at her breast was their newborn child.

"It's a little girl," Jenny said. "A beautiful little girl. Come see her."

Michael knelt by the bed. He could only stare in awe and wonder at the infant nuzzling Jenny's breast.

"Is she going to be all right? Are you OK?" he asked.

"Both of them are doing wonderful," Lucy said. "You can hold her if you wish. Just be careful."

Lucy helped Jenny wrap the infant in a blanket and passed her to Michael. "She's so tiny," he said, as he touched her softly on the face.

"She's too big to throw back," Ned said. He had followed Michael from the shed and was looking over his son's shoulder to admire his new granddaughter. "She's perfect."

"Ah, young Duggan," Old Joe said, looking in through the bedroom door, "there's no doubt but that's a darling baby you and Jenny have for yourselves. She must have gotten her looks from her mother."

"That's enough out of you," Lucy said. "Try to behave yourself for the rest of the day." It was impossible, however, to be cross in the face of the joy spreading through the room.

Michael passed their new daughter back to Jenny and knelt by her side again. He was happier than he had ever been in his life, but tears streamed down his face.

"She's beautiful," he said. "She's the most beautiful thing I ever saw."

"What will we call her?" Jenny asked Michael.

"Do you have anything in mind?"

"I'm not sure," Jenny said. "I had all kinds of names picked out for a boy, but I was kind of thinking about Penney if we had a girl."

"Maybe Penelope is the name you're looking for," Father Quigley said. He had entered the room behind Michael and was as awestruck as the others. "I think Penelope would be very suitable for when she grows into a young woman. You can call her Penney for short."

"I like it. What do you think?" Jenny asked Michael.

"Penelope, Penney, Penney Duggan. I like it," Michael said. "It's perfect."

Within the hour, with Thomas and his wife Marion as godparents, Father Quigley christened the child who had come into the world with help from the little people. She received the rather sophisticated name of Penelope; however, those who loved her and knew her best, would always call her Penney.

Nobody in the room, including Krab, who had missed nothing from his perch in the closet, knew that this was only the first time that the lives of the starrigans and Penney Duggan would be intertwined.

Chapter 3 - Home with the Starrigans

Krab made his exit from the house when Jenny asked to have the window opened to let in some fresh air. He headed back to Little Brook Bottom where he knew Savid and the others would be waiting for his story. This time he didn't hurry. The blizzard had moved on and it was a crisp, clear day. He squinted his eyes against the bright sun, while the frost nipped at his nose. He took his time meandering along the path, listening to the fresh snow scrunch under his feet, and thinking about what had happened.

He shared some of Michael and Jenny's wonder and joy, but he couldn't help thinking about how it nearly didn't happen. So many things had to fall into place.

"What if I hadn't gone out to play in the blizzard, or if I saw Michael before he saw me. I would have just stayed out of sight and none of this would have happened." He trudged along, stopping occasionally just to relish in the splendour of the world around him. "Why did I ever do something so crazy as to follow Michael home? What if Savid had refused to help or if that cat hadn't shown up? I don't understand it."

In due course he reached the secluded valley where Little Brook meandered towards the river. Ambling through the bottom-land towards the starrigans' enclave, he found himself somewhat saddened that his trek was over. He had enjoyed the solitude. Nevertheless, he was eager to share the good news and trotted into the knoll.

"Savid," he called out. "Savid."

"I'm here, I'm here," the old starrigan said. "Stop making such a racket."

"It worked," Krab said. "It was perfect. The baby is a little girl. They called her Penney."

"I'm glad for them," Savid said. "A new baby is a gift to be treasured. The parents are happy?"

"They love her," Krab said. "The medicine you gave me worked right away. Jenny was almost dead."

By then all the starrigans had gathered around. He tried to recount his story and answer their questions at the same time. Eventually, they all heard the story at least once and he would have to answer no more than a couple of hundred questions over the next few days. The efforts of the ordeal were catching up with Krab and he was tired to the bone. Savid saw his weariness and moved him away from the others.

"You need to rest now," she said. "We will talk later."

Savid led him to his burrow where he once again pondered all that had happened, while falling into one of the deepest sleeps of his life. The stars were out again by the time he woke up. He came out of his burrow to find Savid lying near the witchhazel tree on a bed of dry moldow that some of the others had gathered for her. The pale green moss grew in abundance on the spruce trees surrounding the knoll. She was gazing at the night sky.

"The merry dancers are celebrating the child's birth," she said.

Krab looked up and gasped. The entire northern part of the sky was shimmering with shades of red, green, blue, and white. The display hung high in the sky like enormous illuminated curtains swaying in a soft breeze in the winter night.

"What is it?" he asked.

"Another thing we don't understand," Savid said, "but can enjoy."

"Where is everybody?" Krab said.

"Drek found a big patch of marshberries up near the cross-paths. They're all gone to pick some."

"The berries were probably all in Drek's belly before he told anybody about them." He knew his friend was fond of the only fruit that could be found in the dead of winter.

"Sit down," she said. She moved to make room for him. "Do you ever wonder what's up there?"

"Sometimes," Krab said looking at the sky, "but I'm having enough trouble trying to figure out this world."

"If you ever do," Savid said, "come and explain it to me."

Krab turned to her. "Why do we stay away from the people? They seemed good to me. They tried really hard to help Jenny."

"I'll tell it to you, like it was told to me many years ago," Savid said. "Little ones like us have been on this earth since the time humans first appeared. We were not always the same as we are now and we didn't always live here."

"Where did we live?" Krab asked.

"According to the old starrigans," Savid said, "the first of us lived in a land across the ocean that was hot and dry. Many people lived there, too."

"How did we end up here?" Krab asked.

"Well, it took a long time, but the people spread out through many lands. Some became farmers and others became hunters; some lived in small groups while others lived in cities. Our kind spread out with them."

"You mean there are starrigans everywhere?"

"They're not all starrigans, but there are little people all over the world. Most of them keep to themselves. Some became a lot like humans."

"Like humans? I don't understand."

"They fought among themselves and tried to get power over others," Savid said. "They caused trouble for each other and for humans."

"That wasn't very smart," Krab said. "It's dangerous too."

"The worst part was that sometimes the humans saw the little people doing the mischief, and began to fear us."

"Was it crunnocks that caused the trouble?" Krab asked.

"Yes, them and others," Savid said. "But the crunnocks were the worst. They believed that whoever was the strongest was the best."

"That's stupid."

"Maybe so, but it was the main reason the little people and humans grew apart. They hardly ever noticed when we helped them. It was the evil that they remembered."

"Are there any crunnocks around here?" Krab asked.

"No, I don't think so," Savid said. "According to the old legends starrigans and crunnocks lived together on another island across the ocean where the sun comes up every morning."

"We lived with the crunnocks?"

"Yes, but they made life hard for the starrigans. It got so bad that the oldest starrigan in the clan decided to move us to a new land."

"How did that happen?"

"The humans have big ships that they use to cross the ocean. One night the starrigans hid away on one. They spent many days and nights on the ocean." She looked to the stars as she recalled the story. "It was a difficult time. The ship finally reached this island. It stopped not far from here where many people live."

"Did the starrigans stay there very long?"

"We didn't stay at all," Savid said. "On the night the ship stopped, the old starrigan led them away from the people and into the forest. We have lived in these woods ever since."

"How long ago did all this happen?" Krab asked.

"More than three long lifetimes ago," Savid said. "When I was young a very old starrigan told me the story. He heard it when he was young from an old starrigan who was there."

"Was it before the humans came to Pinchgut?" Krab asked.

"I believe they came to Pinchgut about the same time. We never had much to do with them. I think they also remembered stories from the old places and feared us."

"Can't we change that?" Krab asked. "They seem like they are really nice."

"No doubt many of them are," Savid said. "And remember, sometimes we do help them."

Krab smiled. He was so engrossed in Savid's tale that he had forgotten about his own adventure.

"There is no reason why we shouldn't help them when we can," Savid said. "But it's best for us to stay out of sight. Many humans are good, but some are not. They might want to hurt us."

"That's true," Krab said.

The sound of bantering out on the path announced the return of the other starrigans from the berry-picking expedition. Krab stood up to go meet them. Before he left, he turned to Savid with one last question.

"Do you think the crunnocks could ever come here?"

Savid shrugged and said, "Who knows? We did."

Several weeks had come and gone since Penney's birth. The days were longer, and the sunshine had freed the river from the icy cover that locked it down all winter. The only snow still to be found was hidden from the sun behind hills and trees, leaving the slide paths bare and unusable. The men had abandoned their camp in Little Brook Bottom and returned home to Pinchgut. Thousands of logs they had cut were piled on the riverbank waiting for the last vestiges of ice to melt from the sides of the river. Then the woodsmen would come back to roll the logs into the river and drive them downstream to Pinchgut.

Krab and the other starrigans enjoyed this season when the birds returned and new life came to the land. They spent their days meandering along the riverbanks and poking through the forest, all the while rediscovering the world they lived in. One morning Krab was skylarking on the mountains of logs piled by the side of the river when he saw Mot coming towards him.

"What might you be up to this fine morning?" Mot said. "Are you planning to do any more favours for your friends who are cutting our home from around us?" He gestured at the logs.

"Mot, if you had to know what you were talking about before you spoke, you would never be able to open your mouth again," Krab said. "Anyway, there are lots of trees in here for all of us."

"There won't be if they keep cutting as many as they did this winter," Mot said.

"Do you have to complain about everything?"

"Oh, in a bad mood today are we, Krab?" Mot asked. "What's wrong? Do you miss your new baby?"

"There was nothing wrong with me until you showed up, and that's enough to make the river want to run the other way." Krab stood eye to eye with Mot. "What is with you, anyway? Why do you always sound like a crow with a sore head?"

"Because I'm sick and tired of listening to you prating about how wonderful that baby is," Mot said. "It'll grow up to be just like the rest of them. I don't see the need for all the fuss."

"You would if you had been there," Krab said. "She's beautiful."

"Nothing ever had a baby that beautiful," Mot said. "No animal, no fish, no bird—and certainly no human."

"Like I said, Mot, your mouth would never open if you had to know what you were talking about. You'd change your mind pretty fast if you saw her," Krab said.

"In your dreams, Krab," Mot said. "In your dreams. I could look at that youngster all day and nothing would change except that I'd be more certain about how right I am."

"Let's find out then," Krab said. "Let's go see her. That is, if you're not afraid."

"I'm afraid of nothing," Mot said. "If you want me to go see this jewel you've got everybody babbling about, I'll go with you."

"Where are you going?" asked another starrigan. It was Drek. He just came along in time to hear the last part of the exchange. He clambered up on the logs to join them.

"I'm taking Mot to see the baby," Krab said. "He wants to see how beautiful she is, don't you, Mot?"

"Hardly," Mot said. "But I'll go, if it will help put an end to this foolishness. Besides I don't have anything else to do today anyway."

"I'm going, too," Drek said. "This should be fun."

"We can't have a big crowd," Krab said. "We'll never get in the house without someone seeing us."

"Who's getting afraid now?" Mot asked. "I say we worry about that when we get there. What do you think, Drek?"

"All right, all right," Krab said. "We'll all go. But we're not taking anybody else and we're not going to take any chances when we get there. OK?"

"Let's go," both of the others said. With that the three of them bounded down off the logs and scampered along the path that would take them to Pinchgut.

Along the way they stopped in the ridge where Krab first met Michael.

"There was a big snowdrift right there," Krab said. "I jumped out of that tree and he saw me just as I landed." Krab pointed out the locations to the others. "When I looked up he was standing right there where you are now. He was looking right at me."

"Wow, I didn't know he was that close to you," Drek said.

"Neither did I," Krab said. "We can laugh at it now, but it wasn't funny when it happened."

"What did you do then?" Drek asked.

"I went up the tree as fast as I could. See that hole up there? That's the woodpecker's nest that I hid in." Drek and Mot scooted up the tree to explore the nest.

"You were still pretty close to him," Mot said. "It must have been your lucky day, Krab. You could be in a cage now."

"I don't think so," Krab said. "He was more afraid of me than I was of him. He could have found me if he wanted to."

"Maybe so," Mot said, "but I'm glad it was you and not me."

Soon after they set out again they came to Island Pond where Krab retold the story about crossing the pond on Michael's back. The ice was now gone and they had to follow the path around the pond. After a while they arrived at the neat little house in Pinchgut. They hid behind the woodshed while they surveyed the area. The only sign of activity around the house was the laundry on the clothesline. Krab noticed that most of the clothes were tiny and had to belong to Penney.

"Looks as if all of the men are at the mill," Drek said.

"They're getting ready for the log drive," Mot said. "That long chain of logs out in the river is a boom. Those big, square boxes made of logs are cribs." He pointed to where the cribs were lined up across the river. "The men will fill the cribs with rocks and use them to anchor the boom. The boom will catch the logs coming down the river."

"We know all that, Mot," Krab said. "We've seen it before. It looks like a lot of the men are inside the mill."

"More than likely they're just making sure everything is working right for when they get the logs here," Mot said.

Just then Jenny came out through the door with more laundry. She waved to one of the men working in the river as she hung the laundry on the line. He waved back.

"That must be Michael out there," Drek said. "I don't think anybody else is in the house except Jenny and the baby."

"How do we get in?" Drek asked.

"Look's like we won't be able to use the door," Krab said. "She keeps it closed except when she's using it herself. Let's see if there's another way."

"I'll look around," Mot said. "You two stay here." He was back in minutes.

"There's a window open over there," Mot said. It was in the kitchen. "The woman is inside washing more clothes. I couldn't see anybody else."

"Go back and watch her," Krab said. "When she leaves the room we'll go in and find a way to get to the baby's room. Watch for that cat, too. It might still be around."

"Here puss, puss, puss," Mot said, as he went back to the window. Krab and Drek couldn't help but laugh.

"I'd say it's the cat that should be worried," Drek said. "Trying to make a meal out of Mot will really mess up its day."

A few minutes later Mot called out to them. "Come on, she's gone upstairs."

The three starrigans popped into the house and were hiding behind the stove when Jenny came back down the stairs.

As soon as her back was turned the three of them zipped up the stairs and into Penney's room.

"What a difference," said Krab. "Look at how big she is now. The last time I saw her she was wrinkly and her skin was full of red botches."

She spotted the three visitors as soon they landed on her crib. She giggled and tried to reach them.

"Wow!" Drek said. "She's just like you said she was."

"She's beautiful," Krab said. "What do you think now, Mot?"

"Not bad, not bad at all," Mot said. "Watch this."

He jumped up and landed on a mobile hanging over the crib. The mobile, which Ned made for his granddaughter, consisted of a bird, a kitten, and a puppy carved from wood and painted blue, red, and yellow. The animals hung on strings from a wooden hoop.

"Yahoo," Mot said. "Come on you two. Get on."

Penney laughed as she watched the three starrigans ride the bird, kitten, and puppy around and around above her head. When they tired of that they practiced somersaults from the rail to the blankets. Then it was time to play peek-a-boo. Penney loved everything the starrigans did.

"Mot, I think she stole your heart," Krab said.

"It's just as well to have some fun since we came this far," Mot said.

"You're doing more than just having fun," Drek said. "You adore her. Admit it."

Mot just grinned.

"This stuff is good," Drek said. He had found some left-over cereal in a small dish on a stand near the baby's crib.

"All you ever think about is your stomach," Mot said. He was trying to keep Penney's attention to himself by walking around the rail of her crib on his hands. "That's her food. Leave it alone."

The three of them were so engrossed with Penney that they didn't notice the change in Jenny's footsteps as she left the kitchen and began to come up the stairs. It was only when she spoke halfway to the bedroom that they became aware of her.

"How's mommy's little angel now?"

The three starrigans raced for cover. Krab made it to the closet that he already knew so well. Drek managed to get behind the dresser. Mot barely had time to dive under the blanket in Penney's crib. Drek and Krab looked on in horror. If Jenny lifted the blanket she was sure to see him.

"Oh my, you're still awake and you didn't make a sound," Jenny said. "What a little sweetheart you are." She smiled as her daughter stretched her arms out, in anticipation of being picked up. "Oh, I smell something, though. I think you need to be changed, don't you? Mommy will get a nice clean diaper and we'll get you freshened up. That's what we'll do."

Jenny took a clean diaper and some other clothing out of the dresser. Krab and Drek were close to panic. Then, with the baby's clothes in her arms, she reached into the crib and scooped baby Penney out from under the blanket. "We'll go down to the kitchen and make you all nice and clean again. Mommy's little angel, that's what you are," Jenny said, as she carried Penney out of the room.

"Mot, are you all right?" Krab and Drek asked at the same time. They bounded into the crib to find him.

"Air, I need air. Give me room to breathe," he gasped. "That was horrible. I couldn't breathe. I never smelled anything that bad in my life."

Drek and Krab rolled to the floor in laughter as Mot gagged and gasped.

"That's what you get for being so crooked all the time," Krab said.

"Looks good on you, Mot," Drek said. He could barely get his own breath between hoots of laughter.

"I knew no good would ever come of this," Mot grumbled. He watched the other two enjoying themselves at his expense.

It was almost dark that evening before the trio made their way back to the clan at Little Brook Bottom. The other starrigans had a thousand questions about Penney and they tried to answer all of them.

"It's hard to believe how big she's grown," Krab said.

"She's gorgeous," Drek said. "She's the cutest thing I ever saw. She's just like Krab told us."

"She stinks," Mot said—but none of the starrigans expected him to say anything good anyway.

Chapter 4 - The World Changes

As he surveyed Pinchgut from his perch in the old spruce tree, Krab mused about all that had happened over the past few years. Since his memorable excursion with Drek and Mot more than two years ago, he never pushed his luck by going back inside the house again, but he had seen Penney many times. So had most of the other starrigans. She was often outside with Michael and Jenny and had grown into a beautiful and happy little girl. She had coal-black hair and big brown eyes and loved to explore the small, safe world around her home.

Krab could see much of Pinchgut from the tree. The place boasted a couple of dozen homes scattered around the mouth of the river, right where it emptied into a saltwater bay. A long wooden bridge spanned the river just below the mill. On the high tide the water under the bridge was deep enough to be navigated by small craft, but at low tide the water disappeared, leaving the estuary strewn with islands of wet gravel.

The houses were tidy affairs, mostly two-story, peak-roof structures built in roomy yards bordered by white-washed fences. Close by almost every house was a vegetable garden, and beyond the gardens hay-meadows reached back to the woods. Convenient to each dwelling was a woodshed and a wellhouse, while a little farther away stood the stable, henhouse and cellar. Situated somewhere discreetly in among it all was the outhouse.

The boom in front of the sawmill held thousands of logs cut the previous winter. Operations were in full swing. Smoke spewed from the stack that towered above the mill, as the furnace inside devoured the slabs and wood-shavings left over from when the logs were ripped into lumber. The burning slabs and shavings fuelled the steam engine that, in turn, powered the saws. The cycle was relentless, from seven in the morning until six in the evening, Monday to Saturday. The men looked like busy ants going about their labours. Krab watched two of them use pike poles to hook the logs and pull them to where the long ramp from the mill dipped into the river. The haul-up chain was wrapped around the dripping logs and then the wet bundles were pulled up the ramp and into the mill. He could hear the scream of the saws cutting the logs into sweet-smelling lumber. All around the place, children were playing and skylarking in the bright midsummer sun. The bridge that joined both halves of the hamlet was in constant use with people running errands or just outdoors enjoying the warm weather.

Krab saw Penney several times earlier in the day playing in the yard under Jenny's watchful eye. She was indoors for the last hour or so, but came out again while Jenny was hanging clothes on the line. The little girl was engrossed by some robins hunting for worms in the grass around the house. She made exaggerated efforts to sneak up on the birds, but there was a limit as to how close the wary thrushes would allow her to come before they took refuge in the trees. Jenny allowed her to stay in the yard while she went back and forth to the house for more laundry. She was careful to leave the door open so that the little girl could call out if she needed her mother.

Jenny had just gone back inside for the last of her day's wash when Penney ran towards some small trees growing at the edge of the meadow. Krab noted that she was farther away from the house than usual.

"Those robins are going to get her in trouble if she keeps chasing them," Krab thought. He sat upright and watched her cross the meadow until she disappeared among the trees. "I better get rid of them so she'll go back to her house."

He bounded down out of the tree and scampered across the meadow. As he got near Penney's location he realized it wasn't the robins she was chasing. Something jumping and running just behind the trees had her attention.

"What are they doing?" he asked. "They know better than to lead her away from her mother."

Krab didn't know any of the other starrigans were coming to Pinchgut today, and he was more than a little upset to see two of them leading Penney well beyond where Jenny considered safe. He ran to tell them to get away before they caused trouble for themselves or Penney. He reached a patch of blueberry bushes growing along the edge of the meadow and was about to yell at the two scallywags when he stopped dead in his tracks.

The little people luring Penney away from the yard were complete strangers to him. At first glance they looked similar to the starrigans that he had known all his life, but there were some very noticeable differences. They were trying to keep Penney's attention by jumping and running around, but their actions were not at all playful. They were rough and combative as they pushed and shoved each other. Both looked fierce and sounded quarrelsome. Around their middles each wore a belt that looked like it was made from some kind of rope. The belts held wooden clubs.

"Crunnocks," Krab gasped. He dived for cover into the blueberry bushes.

Krab watched in horror as the two crunnocks led the giggling and laughing little girl farther into the woods.

"Oh, what can I do?" Krab asked. "Jenny, where are you?"

By now Penney had followed the pair out of sight of the house. Krab ran into the woods behind them, careful to remain unseen. He watched the villains confer with each other for a moment, and then one of them scampered up into a small tree and out on a limb above the little girl's head. She laughed and jumped trying to reach him.

"What's he doing?" Krab asked.

It soon became clear.

The crunnock snatched the sunbonnet from Penney's head and threw it to his companion. The second one raced back towards the house with the bonnet. While his partner kept Penney's attention and continued to lead her farther away, the crunnock with the bonnet carried the little hat down over the bank and threw it in the river. Then he scampered back to join his cohort.

Jenny was only in the house for a few minutes before she came out again with her arms full of clothes to hang on the clothesline.

"Penney, where are you?" she called. "Penney, come here now." Jenny was puzzled and somewhat annoyed as she laid down the laundry and began to look for her daughter. "Penney, if you're hiding I want you to come out right now."

Her concern grew and she ran around all sides of the house. She opened the shed door and looked inside but there was no trace of her little girl. By the time she looked through the garden and behind the woodpile she was beginning to panic, but it was only when she ran along where the fence overlooked the river that she was seized with complete and utter terror. She saw Penney's sunbonnet floating in the water. She fell over the fence and stumbled down to the river screaming for her daughter.

"Penney! Penney! Where are you? Penney!"

She ran, still screaming, into the river and grabbed the little hat. Frantically, she raced up and down the river, slipping and falling on the slimy rocks, but there was no sign of her little girl.

Across the river several men were working outside in the millyard, but they couldn't hear Jenny's cries over the din from the wood saws. Michael's younger brother, Edmund, the same one who had fetched the priest on the night that Penney was born, was marking and packing lumber as the trolley-cars brought it out of the mill. Straightening up from where he was bent over a stack of two-by-fours, he glanced towards his brother's house, only to see Jenny stumbling around in the river.

"What the—" he started to say before yelling to the others working alongside him. "Something's wrong! Get some help!"

Edmund charged across the bridge and out into the river on the other side.

"What's wrong?" he yelled.

"I can't find Penney! She's gone! I can't find her!"

Word spread quickly through the mill, and the entire crew, more than twenty men, dropped what they were doing and ran to assist. They were all close on Edmund's heels. Michael was among those at the front of the group.

"Mike, she can't find Penney," Edmund cried. "Everybody spread out!"

"How did she get in the river?" Michael asked, trying to get some sense from his hysterical wife. "Maybe she's still in the house."

"I found this in the river," Jenny cried. She pushed the little sunbonnet into her husband's hands. "Mike, find her. Please, find her for me. Don't let me lose her."

"We'll find her," Michael said. "Don't worry. She's around here somewhere."

By then Michael's father had reached the river and was taking control of the search.

"Mike, take Jenny up to the house and go through the place with a fine-tooth comb. A couple of you go with Michael. Check the shed and the wellhouse." Ned barked orders like a general. "Three or four of you young fellows go to the saltwater as fast as you can and work your way back here. The rest of you spread out in a straight line and cover the whole river. Get a couple of dories and row out underneath the bridge. Look everywhere."

The women of Pinchgut began to show up as well. They had noticed the rhythm of the mill changing and then stopping altogether in midday. Seeing their men running to the river told them that the problem wasn't mechanical. The first woman to reach the river was Michael's mother, Sues Duggan. She ran out into the water and took Jenny's arm to lead her back to shore.

"Jenny, come in out of the water," she said. "It's going to be all right. We'll find her."

"Let me go. I have to find her. Let me go." Jenny broke away from Sues.

"Jenny, my love, come here. We'll find her." Sues managed to get her arms around Jenny again. "She's not down here. Look, the tide is out. There's hardly any water."

"Where is she? My God, where is she?" Jenny cried.

"She's probably still up by the house" Sues said. "There are lots of people here now. Don't worry, we'll find her. Come up to the house with me."

"Did they look in the house?" Jenny asked. "Is she there?"

"They're looking in the house now," Sues said. "Don't worry. You come with me."

Jenny twisted and turned, looking in all directions as Sues led her back to her house. Her cries could be heard all through Pinchgut. "Where is she? Penney! Penney, where are you?"

Krab was dismayed to see that the strategy of deception used by the conniving crunnocks had worked perfectly. Penney and her abductors were now a considerable distance from the house and well out of range of the initial search. To make matters worse, the two scoundrels continued to delight the little girl with their  antics, and she hurried after them, all the while getting farther and farther away from her would-be rescuers.

Every able-bodied soul in the tiny community was soon involved in the search. Old Joe O'Reilly was in the meadow behind Penney's house. He was trying to catch up with Ned Duggan.

"Ned, wait up."

"What is it, Joe? Did you find something?"

"She's not in the house or in the yard," Old Joe said. "I got a few of the men to string fishing nets right across the river. Nothing can get out under the bridge. What are you doing now?"

"I'm going back down to check the river again," Ned said. "I want to make sure we look in all the holes and around the rocks."

"That's already been done, Ned. She's not down there." He placed his big bony hand on Ned's shoulder and turned him towards the river. "Look, the tide has been out for hours. The water is only up to your knees."

"I know, but where else could she be?" Ned asked. "A child can't just disappear into thin air. I'm going to have another look around the meadow."

"I'll do that," Old Joe said. "You can do more good in the house. Jenny is in a bad way. See if you can do anything for her."

"I probably should send for Father Quigley," Ned said.

"Lucy told me that Sues already sent one of the young fellows with a note for him to come here as quick as he can," Old Joe said. "You need to go see her now and try to make her feel better."

"Finding Penney is the only thing that will do that," Ned said.

"Well, convince her that we *will* find her," Old Joe said. "Tell her we won't stop until we do."

"All right. I'll see what I can do. I'll see you in a little while."

"I'll be here."

Old Joe stood alone in the middle of the meadow and looked around. He could see Michael and some others still searching near the house. More men were poking into and under every building and outbuilding in Pinchgut. Women and children walked the riverbank and spread out through the gardens. A great effort was being made, but there was no sign of the little girl. He stared at the woods across the river. After a little while he rooted in his pockets for his pipe and tobacco pouch. He filled the pipe and lit it. When he had it going to his satisfaction he gazed around the place once more, and then looked skyward.

"I'm thinking this is going to get worse before it gets better," he said.

The two crunnocks avoided the beaten trails. They lured Penney into the thick woods, away from the places likely to be searched first. The ground was dry and they left no tracks. Within the first hour they led her almost a mile from her house. That distance more than doubled by the time the sun made its crimson descent in the western sky, setting the searchers to making torch lights so they could continue their efforts after dark.

Penney was getting tired by then, and the novelty of the crunnocks' antics was wearing thin. It was also well past her mealtime. She was hungry and wanted her mom and dad. She had been led to a part of the woods where the trees were large and grew close together. It was impossible to see any farther than the distance a man could walk in a dozen steps. The thick evergreen foliage and constant breeze of the summer evening muted any cries that she might make, none of which were relevant anyway, since the search was focused nowhere near her. She balked at going any farther and sat down on the dry moss among some scarlet crackerjack berries. She ignored the crunnocks as they tried to entice her to follow them farther, and angrily brushed them aside when they tugged on her smock to get her to move.

Krab watched it all.

"Good girl, Penney," he thought. "Don't do anything for those sleeveens. I don't know how to get you back home yet, but I'll figure out something."

He was close enough to hear them talking. He was surprised that they spoke the same language as he did, except they had a strange accent and used words he had not heard before. It made sense. He recalled Savid's explanation about how they had all lived together at one time. He was able to get the gist of much of what they were saying.

"I'd like to see someone top this, Ral. They all talk about what they're going to do, but we did it."

"Drog, we haven't done anything yet. Yes, we did get her to follow us here; but we still have to get her to Sor before the people find her."

"We'll do it," Drog said. "We got her this far. We'll get her the rest of the way."

"Maybe," Ral said. "But she's not moving very fast now."

"She will," Drog said. "Come on. Come with me." He tugged at Penney's dress but she wouldn't move. "Come on. Why are you being so hard to get along with now?"

"Maybe she's tired," Ral said. "Let her sit here for a few minutes. I'll watch her. You go back the way we came to make sure nobody followed us."

"Nobody saw us," Drog said. "How could they follow us?"

"They might be tracking her," Ral said. "They have dogs, you know. Get out there and check to make sure they're not coming after us."

"All right," Drog said. "I'll go, if it will make you happy."

Drog disappeared through the undergrowth. Ral turned his attention back to Penney. She was still sitting on the ground, munching on berries. He walked all around her. "Well, my treasure, how are we going to get you moving again?"

She paid him no heed, until he pulled on her leg in an effort to get her moving again. She lashed out with her other foot. He jumped backwards just in time to avoid her boot.

"Watch it, will you! You don't have to kick me. I'm only trying to get you out of these woods."

Krab was hiding in the nearby undergrowth and saw Penney's anger with Ral. He smiled for the first time since the crisis started.

"Keep it up, Penney," he thought. "Put the boots to him. If you can get rid of one of them, I might be able to handle the other one." He looked to see if there was any sign of Drog. Nothing yet. "But, then again, that would be a pretty stupid thing to try. If anything happens to me she might never get home."

He squirmed farther down in the undergrowth and continued to watch. He remembered Savid's words from the night Penney was born. *If it is meant that we should help, a way will present itself.*

Ral was still looking at Penney. She glared back at him.

"You don't like us anymore, do you? That's too bad because you're stuck with us until we get you to Sor. You may as well get up and start walking again."

"Who are you talking to?" Drog asked, as he reappeared through the bushes.

"Her, myself—I don't know who I'm talking to anymore," Ral said. "Did you see anything?"

"Not a thing," Drog said. "Nobody's following us. She won't move yet?"

"She's worse," Ral said. "We might be stuck here with her all night."

"It's probably just as well," Drog said. "There's no way we can get her to Sor tonight and the people will never find her here."

"I don't like it," Ral said. "We're not far enough away yet. The people can get here in no time."

"They're not even looking this way," Drog said. "You saw them. They're still out by the river and around the houses."

"We'll see what we can do," Ral said. "She might be easier to get along with later." He was near Penney, but was careful to stay out of her reach.

Penney filled her tummy with the sweet crackerjack berries that grew in bunches and were easy, even for her, to pick by the handful. The evening was warm and the wind blew a soft lullaby through the trees.

"Oh no," Ral said. "Look at her now. She's falling asleep."

Penney was stretched out on the warm ground, her eyes rolled back in her head. In no time at all, she was in a sound slumber.

"Well," Drog said, "it looks like she made that decision for us."

"You want to know something?" Ral asked. "We'll never live long enough to bring her to Sor."

"Why not?"

"Look at her, you chucklehead," Ral said. "She was in good shape today. She wanted to come with us and we only got this far."

"Don't call me a chucklehead," Drog said. "This was your idea, too. What do you want to do?"

"You'll have to get Sor and bring him here," Ral said. "I'll wait with her."

"We can't split up," Drog said. "Some of the others will be around here tomorrow. We can send them for Sor."

"It might be days before any of them come here," Ral said. "They may never show up. You go get Sor."

"I'm not going anywhere," Drog said. "I'm staying here with you and her."

"You're just afraid to go back by yourself. You're afraid of the dark. You're afraid the boogeyman might get you."

"I'm not afraid of anything," Drog said. "I can go anywhere I want to."

"You're afraid to leave my sight," Ral said. "It makes no difference anyway. Sor wouldn't listen to you."

"Sor will listen to me," Drog said, "and I'm not afraid."

"Yeah, right," Ral said. "Talk is cheap."

"I'll prove it," Drog said. "You watch and see. I'll bring them all back." With that he lit out through the woods.

"Chucklehead," Ral said, watching him go. "Anyway, I'm glad I don't have to face that hike tonight." He looked at Penney, who was sound asleep. "For a while there, I wasn't sure I could talk him into going. Sor is going to be pleased to see you—and pleased with me."

He lay down on the warm ground to wait for his clan. The exertions of the day, the warmth of the evening, and the thoughts of glory to come, soon lulled him into a deep delicious slumber.

Chapter 5 - Helping Out Again

Krab watched Drog leave and then waited, concealed in the green shrubs at the edge of the glade, until Ral fell asleep.

"This might be my chance," he thought. "If I can get some help before the rest of the crunnocks get here, we should be able to take Penney away from them. I have to get to Little Brook Bottom." He made note of Penney's exact location and then sped off. He was racing around Island Pond when he spotted some other starrigans in the middle of the marsh. It was Drek and Mot, along with a few more from their clan, picking bakeapple berries.

"Mot, Drek, come here," he yelled. He rushed out on the marsh.

"What's wrong, Krab?" Drek asked.

"Crunnocks—in Pinchgut," Krab said. "They got Penney. We have to help her."

"Are you gone loony?" Mot asked. "There are no crunnocks around here. You've been listening to too many of Savid's stories."

"They are here," Krab said. "I saw them and they got Penney. We have to help her."

"You're serious, aren't you?" Mot asked.

"Yes," Krab said. "They took her out of her yard. I followed them."

"Where is she now?" Drek asked. "How many crunnocks are there?"

"There are two of them. No, there's only one now," Krab said. "The other one is gone to get the rest of them. They have Penney in the woods between here and Pinchgut."

"Only one," Mot said. "Show me where. Drek, you go and tell Savid what's going on. The rest of you come with me."

Drek took off immediately for Little Brook Bottom. Krab and Mot and the other berry-pickers rushed back to where Penney and Ral were asleep. They approached the site quietly.

"See him," Krab said. "He's still asleep."

"I see him," Mot said, "but I don't believe it. It is a crunnock. Any sign of the rest of them?"

"Not yet," Krab said. "What will we do?"

"We can just wake her up and take her now," Soc said. "She must miss her mommy and daddy. If the crunnock wakes up, we can tie him to a tree."

"Then we can bring her close to home where her people will find her," another known as Nak said. "There's not much one crunnock can do against all of us."

"It's not going to be easy," Mot said.

"You don't want anything to be easy," Nak said. "What's so hard about it?"

"I'm just thinking this through," Mot said. "If we tie up laddie-buck and leave him here, he can tell the other crunnocks we are around here somewhere, and that we have Penney with us. We don't know how many of them there are, or if we can get her home before they show up."

"You're right," Krab said. "What do you think we should do, then?"

"We either have to get her away without him knowing it, and that's impossible," Mot said, "or we have to take him with us."

"Take him with us?" the others said. "Have you lost your mind? That's crazy."

"If we leave him here the other crunnocks will come after us and try to take her back," Mot said. "That won't happen if they don't know anything about us. We have to take him."

"Mot's right," Krab said.

"OK, so how will we do it?" Soc asked.

"Stay close to me and help me when I need it," Mot said. He led them to where Ral and Penney were sleeping. Mot approached the crunnock the same way he approached most things in life—head on.

"Get up you useless lout," Mot yelled. At the same time he administered a well-aimed kick to Ral's ribs. The crunnock bellowed in surprise and rage. He tried to jump to his feet. Mot's fist met him halfway and sent him crashing back to the ground. "Who do you think you are? Coming here and taking our little girl away from her home. I'm going to send you back to wherever you came from."

The crunnock rolled away and staggered to his feet. "Starrigans? Come here. See what I have for you." He pulled his club from his belt and waved it at Mot.

"You're threatening me?" Mot roared.

The other starrigans stood with mouths agape as Mot swatted the club out of Ral's hand as if he was brushing away an annoying insect. Once, twice, three times, he delivered open-handed smacks across the ears of the muddled crunnock. Ral was defenceless against the fury of the starrigan's onslaught.

"Take our little girl, will you? Wave that thing in my face? I'll fix you so that if any part of you isn't hurting, you'll think it fell off."

The crunnock cowered under the attack and the fight was over without really getting started.

"Stop, stop, enough," Ral said.

Mot stood over him ready to give him more if he made the slightest wrong move. The others stood there. Finally Krab spoke up.

"Mot, you just let us know when you're ready for help," he said.

"See if you can wake Penney," Mot said. "One of you give me a hand with this nuisance." He was a little winded from his exertions.

Mot and Nak used Ral's belt to bind his hands behind his back. Mot took a moment to examine Ral's club. Since he had no use for the weapon himself, he gave Ral a tap on the nose, and then threw the club into the woods. Krab and the others were busy trying to get Penney awake. They pulled on her hair and tried to pry open her eyelids, but she was still drowsy from the long walk. Finally, she sat up and rubbed her eyes.

"Maybe the best thing to do is for a couple of us to get him away from here and the rest of us can look after her," Soc said.

"That'll probably be best," Nak said.

"Nak, you and me will take this fellow to Little Brook Bottom," Mot said. "Savid can figure out what to do with him. The rest of you stay with Penney and try to keep her away from the crunnocks."

"We have to get her far enough away so that the crunnocks can't find her when they come back," Krab said.

"They'll think she's trying to get home," Mot said, "and start searching between here and Pinchgut. I'd say it's best to keep her safe first and get her home later."

"We need to find out more about the crunnocks," Krab said. "A couple of us should hide here until they come back. We have to know their strengths and weaknesses."

"I'll stay," one said.

"Me too," said another.

"Be careful," Soc said. "I don't want anything to happen to either of you."

"Don't worry. They won't see us."

Mot and Nak headed towards Little Brook Bottom with Ral in tow. The crunnock was dumfounded by the turn of events. It was dark before Krab, Soc and the others managed to get Penney moving. Soc stayed closer to the little girl than any of the other starrigans. The little girl seemed to sense the compassion in the kind-hearted starrigan and wanted to be close to her. As Soc beckoned for Penney to follow them, the child reached down and picked up the little starrigan. She carried Soc like a doll while the others stayed close by.

Krab led the way. Making his way through the darkness, he realized that these strangers had changed the starrigans' lives forever.

Darkness falling over Pinchgut brought new urgency to the search. Every man, woman, and child, who could physically help out was doing so. The river and its banks were swept from the saltwater to the horseshoe-shaped bend called the Crow's Nest more than a mile upriver. All houses were searched, inside and outside. Horses, cows, and sheep were evicted, so their stalls and mangers could be examined. Wellhouses were opened up allowing searchers to peer into the depths of the still water inside. Hens and roosters were turned out and the henhouses swept for signs of the child. Dogs had to leave their houses to let searchers enter. Even the outhouses in Pinchgut were searched, re-searched, and then searched twice again. Penney was nowhere to be found.

Father Quigley came to Pinchgut as soon as he was notified of the crisis. He had spent most of the time since his arrival with Jenny. Now he was standing on a chair to light one of the kerosene lamps mounted on the wall of the little building that served as a school and a church. Now, it would serve as the headquarters for the search. Two women from Pinchgut were with him. They were setting up tables and getting ready to provide meals for the searchers.

"Do you think we have enough tables, Father?" asked one.

"Plenty, Alice," the priest said. "Only a few of the men are likely to be here at one time. We can set up more if we need them."

"I see three more men coming in the road," another said. "My heavens, they're coming from everywhere. I don't know how the word spread so fast."

"I'm glad it did, Mae," Father Quigley said. "We can use every man we can get. Please God, they'll find her soon."

"I don't understand it, Father," Alice said. "How any mother could let her baby wander away is beyond me."

"Alice Lastner," Mae said, "what a horrible thing to say. Jenny didn't let her child wander off. She disappeared when Jenny turned her back for a moment." Mae put down the dishes she had in her hand and looked at Alice. "Jenny looks after her little one as good as you or I ever looked after our own."

"Well," Alice said, "we never lost either one of ours."

"Alice," said Father Quigley, "that little girl means the world to Jenny. I was there the night she was born, and I just spent the last three hours trying to give her strength to cope with this. She's beside herself with grief."

"The only thing that will help is getting Penney back," Mae said. "Father, how is young Michael?"

"I didn't get a chance to talk to him. He's too busy with the search. It's safe to say, though, he isn't any better than Jenny."

"My heart goes out to the two of them," Alice said. "But I still think this should never have happened."

Mae was about to respond to Alice again when the door opened and three men walked in.

"Hello, Father. Ladies, how are you?" the first to enter asked. He took off his cap in the priest's presence. His companions did likewise. "We saw the light and figured it would be best to come here first to find out what's going on. Have they found the little girl yet?"

"Not yet, my son," the priest responded. "Have you been travelling long?"

"A few hours," the newcomer said. "We're from Riverhead. We came as soon as we heard the news."

"Bless you," the priest said.

"More fellows will come tomorrow unless we go back and tell them the little one is home." They began to unload food-stuffs from their backpacks. "Our women sent along some grub to help feed everyone."

From their knapsacks they took loaves of homemade bread, bottles of rabbit, and a huge ham. Alice and Mae laid the provisions on a table in the corner. It was already piled high with crocks of jam, bread, cakes, and two huge boilers of soup.

"Thank you," Mae said. "This won't be wasted if people keep showing up like they have so far. At least fifteen or twenty men came here in the last couple of hours."

"You fellows sit down and have something to eat," Father Quigley said. "You must be exhausted."

"We didn't come here to eat, Father. There'll be lots of time for that after the child is found. Now, tell us what's going on, and how we can help, and we'll get to it."

"Come outside," Father Quigley said. "I'll show you." The three men followed the priest outside. "That's her house, right there. That's the last place that anybody saw her."

"Have they found any trace of her?" one of the men asked.

"Her bonnet was in the river. The tide was out and there was almost no water, so the men are pretty sure she didn't drown." He pointed to the torchlights on the roads and in the meadows. "You can see where everybody is looking. I suggest you just join up with some of them and go from there."

"Thanks, Father. That's what we'll do." With that, all three men disappeared into the still night air.

Father Quigley gazed around the little hamlet. Men in dories were monitoring the fishing nets strung across the river. The flickering of lights in the distant woods showed the expanding parameters of the search. The windows in all of the houses were aglow and the priest knew the doors were unlocked, so that no matter which doorstep a lost child found her way to, she would find a welcome waiting for her.

"It's impossible for them not to find her," he thought. "A child can't just disappear into thin air. We're overlooking something, but for the life of me I don't know what it is." His people looked to him to explain things they didn't understand. Often, he felt overwhelmed by the task. He expected such would be the case tonight. "This makes no sense, no sense at all."

"You sure you know where you're going, Krab?"

"Nuf, I know I'm going in a straight line," Krab said. "I just hope the line is going where I want it to."

"How can you be sure you're even going straight?" Nuf said.

"Savid showed me. See the Big Dipper? The two stars on the end of the Dipper always point towards the same star. It's the North Star." Krab pointed it out. "Savid says that navigators have used it for thousands of years."

"You're no navigator, Krab," Nuf said.

"I know. But if I keep the North Star ahead of me and a little bit to the right, it should lead us to Island Pond River."

"I hope it works," Nuf said.

"So do I, Nuf. So do I," Krab said. "Soc, how is Penney doing?"

"Not so good," Soc said. "She'll never get far in this tuck-amore bush. It's too much of a tangle. We're going to have to go out on the open barrens." They all stopped.

"I guess it's safe out there," Krab said. "I don't think the crunnocks will come this way tonight."

"What about the people?" Nuf said. "They're going to be looking everywhere for Penney."

The others all stared at him.

"Think about what you're asking, Nuf," Soc said. "It would be like a dream come true if one of the people would see her right now."

"Oh yeah," Nuf said. "That's right." The others laughed at his oversight.

"Come on, let's go out on the barrens," Krab said. "We'll make better time and we'll be out of sight before dawn. Soc, do you think she'll make it?"

"She's all right as long as she has me in her arms and can see the rest of us," Soc said. "She's so sweet. It breaks my heart to think anyone would ever want to hurt her."

They worked their way out to the barrens where their progress would be much better. Their goal was Island Pond River. The starrigans knew dense woods lined its banks; beyond the woods, open marshes would allow the starrigans to see anything approaching—good or bad—from a considerable distance. A perfect hiding place.

It was an unhappy prisoner that Mot and Nak were leading to a different place at the same time. Ral said little as they travelled. He was a slow learner, but he did eventually figure out that Mot intended to respond to all of his complaints by dusting his ears with the back of his hand. They were at the crosspaths at the edge of the barrens above Little Brook Bottom when Mot stopped. He took Nak aside so that Ral couldn't hear them.

"I don't like the idea of letting any of them know where we live," Mot said. "We might be sorry for it before this is all over."

"What do you want to do?" Nak asked.

"We're at the cross-paths," Mot said. "Some of the others are bound to pass along here soon. We can send word to Savid that we have this fellow here and she can let us know what to do with him."

"Makes sense," Nak said. "What will we do while we're waiting?"

"I have an idea. Play along with me." They walked back to where Ral waited for them. "We're going to wait for the cook here."

"Cook?" asked Ral. "What are you going to cook?"

"You," Mot said. He winked at Nak. "You didn't think we hauled your mangy carcass all the way in here for the pleasure of your company, did you?"

"You can't be serious. He's not serious, is he?" the crunnock asked Nak.

"Up to him," Nak said, still trying to figure out what Mot was up to. "He caught you. He decides what to do with you."

"But he can't cook me and eat me," Ral shouted in horror. "Starrigans don't do that, do they? That's crazy!"

"Cook you, yes," Mot said. "Eat you—not if I was starving. The nippers will do the eating. We find if we put something out for them to eat, they leave us alone." He walked behind Ral and checked to make sure the crunnock's bindings were secure. "Cooking dries the meat out and makes it last longer. Cuts down the smell, too."

Nak was trying hard to keep a straight face.

"You can't do that to me. I'll do anything you want. I'll be your slave," Ral said.

"I don't know," Mot said. "The nippers have been giving us a pretty rough time this summer. Everybody will be awfully happy with us if we can get rid of them."

"But . . . but . . . please! You can't do this to me!"

"Sure we can," Mot said. "We can do anything we like with you, and I can't think of anything better right now than turning you into nipper food. What about you, Nak?"

"Uh, I can't think of anything right off the top of my head," Nak said. He was careful to keep his face turned away from their prisoner.

"But I can help you," Ral said. "I can tell you about the other crunnocks. I'm no good if you cook me. Please, let me help you."

Mot paused for a moment. Then he put his arm around Ral's shoulders and smiled at him. "I'll tell you what. You convince me you're worth keeping and, maybe, I'll have a chat with the cook. Let's start with the simple things like . . . oh, let me see. Where are they? And how many are there?"

The rest of the crunnocks were, in fact, quite some distance from Pinchgut. It was long after dark before Drog reached them. Plenty of time, had they known it, for the starrigans to take Penney straight home.

The crunnocks' camp was located in a cove on the eastern side of a saltwater bay. The cove was protected from the ocean by a sandbar, creating a lagoon the local people called a barasway. At the end of the barasway, farthest from the ocean, grew a thicket of tough spruce trees. The constant assault from the cold ocean wind, combined with poor salty soil, stunted the trees' growth. As a result, thousands of trees that should have grown to reach the sky grew, instead, into a twisted tangle barely as high as a man's shoulders. They were impenetrable by anything larger than a rabbit, and it was in the middle of this copse the crunnocks had established camp.

"Sor," Drog yelled. "Sor, where are you?" He rushed into the camp, only to trip over a root and fall flat on his face. Ignoring the laughter of the others, he got up and ran to where a crowd was gathered around a crunnock sitting in the fork of a tree. "Sor, you're not going to believe this."

"But you're going to tell me anyway, aren't you?" the crunnock said. The crunnocks surrounding him laughed again. Drog pushed through them and stood in front of Sor.

"Me and Ral took one of the people's young ones," he said. "We hid her in the woods. All of the people from Pinchgut are looking for her, but they'll never find her, not where we have her."

A hush came over the group. Sor stepped down from his throne and stood nose to nose with Drog. He was larger than the other crunnocks, but not by much. Like Drog, they all wore a belt, but Sor's was more elaborate than the others. The club in his belt was larger and more polished, and he wore a gold-coloured collar around his neck.

"You and Ral better not be wasting my time with some crazy story you cooked up," he said. "Where are they?"

"Ral is still with her. We got her in the woods on the other side of the place with the mill." He gestured towards Pinchgut. "I told him to stay there with her, so that I could come and get you."

"I'm glad to see that Ral followed your orders," Sor said, drawing more guffaws from the clan. "Do the people know you have her?"

"That's the best part, Sor," Drog said. "They're going out of their minds looking for her. They're searching the river and the woods, they're searching everywhere."

"They're still out now, in the dark, looking for her?" Sor said.

"Yes," Drog said. "It's almost too good to be true. You have to come and see it right away."

"I'll decide what I have to do and when I have to do it," Sor said. "Maybe I will go. Maybe I won't. Tell me the whole story."

By then, all of the crunnocks had gathered, more than a hundred in total, to listen while Drog told his story to Sor. He was so excited, he left out many of the details, allowing the others to ask numerous questions. Most of them wanted to trip him up and cast doubt on the story, but to their chagrin, he was able to answer every question they threw at him. Sor finally concluded the story was worth investigating.

"You're not smart enough to make this up," he said. "All right everybody, listen to me." Sor stood so that the whole clan could see him. "Get ready to move. We're going to see the prize that our friends have landed."

"I'll show you the way," Drog said. He stayed by Sor's side as the clan moved en masse out of the barasway. "This is what everyone always talked about doing, but I did it."

"You mean, you and Ral, don't you?" Sor asked.

"Oh yeah, that's right," Drog said. "Ral helped me."

Chapter 6 - The Second Day

Chaos erupted in Little Brook Bottom when Drek delivered the news about the appearance of the crunnocks.

"Savid, what will we do?" the starrigans cried. "What are they going to do to us? Do you think they'll stay here?"

"All of you listen to me," she said. "I'm not happy they're here, but I'm not at all surprised. It's not the end of the world."

"But Savid, they're crunnocks. They hate us."

"We don't know they hate us," Savid said. "We know very little about them. They might cause us some difficulty, but we'll handle it."

"Maybe we should move and find another place to live."

"And abandon Penney?" Savid asked. "We're not going anywhere. Our history has been long and often difficult, but we always survived—and we will now."

"What should we do?"

"Nothing," she said. "Drek said only two crunnocks have been seen. Krab, Mot and the others are trying to get Penney away from them. It's best for now to wait and see what happens, and to learn as much as we can."

"We can't just wait."

"We stay put," Savid said. "We don't know where Krab and the others are, and it's useless to go running around the country looking for them. They'll send word of what's happening and what they want us to do."

Savid, as usual, had things figured out perfectly. A few hours before dawn, Krab led the other starrigans, along with Penney, into a cosy glade on the side of Island Pond River. The thick woods surrounding the clearing provided excellent camouflage, but also enabled the starrigans to see anything approaching.

"We made it," Krab said. "She should be safe here."

"The poor thing is exhausted," Soc said. "Just look at her." The little girl had plopped down in the tall grass. "She'll be asleep in no time."

Soc was right. The tiring hike and the warm air lulled Penney into a deep slumber as soon as she lay down.

"She's going to be asleep for hours," Krab said. "One of us will have to go to Little Brook Bottom before daylight to tell Savid and Mot where we are and to let them know that we're safe." He peered out at the barrens through the trees. "The rest of us will have to take turns standing watch. I'll take the first shift."

"I'll go to Little Brook Bottom," Nuf said. "What do you want me to tell Savid?"

"Just tell her we're all right and we plan to stay put until we hear from her," Krab said.

"Tell her I want to stay with Penney until we get her home," Soc said. "She likes me and she needs a friend now."

"Anything else?" Nuf asked. "No? All right then, I'm on my way." The others watched him go. Then they looked at Penney.

"We'll have to pick some berries for her as soon as it gets light," Soc said.

"We have a lot of work ahead of us," Krab said.

At the cross-paths, on the marshes above Little Brook Bottom, the subject of something to eat or, rather, the fear of becoming something to eat, had Ral's mouth running. On the few occasions when he did stop talking, Mot found simply alluding to the cook motivated him to start again. The more Ral talked, however, the more Mot became convinced he had captured the crunnocks' pet idiot.

"How many crunnocks are there?" Ral had no concept of numbers, so he could only show how much space all of them would take up. Mot figured there were about the same number of crunnocks as starrigans.

"Where are they?" That way.

"How far?" Not too far, but farther away than the three of them travelled during the night.

"What are their plans?" Ral didn't know. Mot didn't doubt him.

"What were you going to do with Penney?" Show her to Sor.

"Then what?" Sor would decide.

"Why was Sor the leader?" Because he was.

And on it went. Mot looked at Nak.

"It sounds like their clan is about the same size as ours," Mot said. "Where do you think they are?"

"As far as I can figure, they're in one of the barasways down along the shore," said Nak. "It's hard to tell which one. What do you make of that fellow 'Sor' he keeps talking about?"

"He sounds like the brains of the bunch," Mot said, "but I don't think he has a lot of competition."

"Chances are, the whole lot of them are on their way to Pinchgut by now," Nak said.

"Yeah, I know," Mot said.

He was just about to ask Nak to go to Little Brook Bottom with the information they had pried from Ral, and to get Savid's advice, when they spotted a starrigan scampering towards them across the barrens. It was Nuf, on his way from Island Pond River. Mot hailed him and was relieved to learn Penney and the other starrigans were safe for the time being. Nuf stopped for a minute before hurrying on to find Savid.

"Ask her what we should do with this fellow," Ral called after him.

"I will," Nuf said.

Not long after Krab and the other starrigans arrived at Island Pond River, the clan of crunnocks, with Drog strutting by Sor's side, reached the outskirts of Pinchgut. They waited there for the sun to rise so they could see what was happening. It was soon bright enough to get a good look all around the place. Some searchers stayed out all night, and at daylight dozens more joined them as the full-scale search resumed.

"See what I told you?" Drog said. "They're still going mad."

"Look at them, Sor," one of his cronies said. "They're frantic. They must've been on the go all night."

"Wow," another said. "They're really upset about something. Drog and Ral really got them going, didn't they, Sor?"

Sor only grunted.

"See, I told you, Sor," said Drog. "They can't find her. I bet you never saw anything like this before did you?"

"You got them a bit bothered," Sor said. "Not a bad start, considering it was only you and Ral. I think we'll spook them a little bit more before we leave." He called the assembly of scoundrels into a huddle.

Minutes later a horse bolted from its stable. Then, as if on cue, every animal in the place began—as one witness later described it—to go nuts. In ordinary times, it would have been a source of puzzlement, maybe even humour, but this was no ordinary morning. All around the little town the people clutched one another as they watched the frightened animals.

"What's going on?" a woman called to her neighbour.

"I don't know. Look at them. They're scared to death," the neighbour said.

"Even the dogs are running. What's happening to them?"

"They must see something we can't. There's something here, something evil."

"Don't be so foolish."

"What then? First a child is gone, now this. Can you tell me what it is?"

"I don't know. I never saw anything like it in my life."

They never suspected a nuisance like Sor had frightened the horse as a signal to the other crunnocks, dispersed throughout Pinchgut moments earlier, to frighten every animal they could find.

One person not frightened by the bolting animals was Old Joe O'Reilly. He was standing in the meadow behind Penney's house talking to Ned when it happened. Old Joe was a driver. He pushed everyone around him to their limits, but he drove himself hardest of all. His commanding physical presence was equalled by his sound mind, and it was to Old Joe that Ned Duggan and the other community leaders turned for advice and guidance.

Ned was relieved when, just at sunrise, he saw Old Joe coming out of the woods. He went out into the meadow to meet him. As the search had progressed through the previous evening and into the night, Ned found he was beginning to doubt his own judgment. He expected Penney would have been found long before this, and the fear that he was overlooking something was growing. He could use Joe's wise counsel.

"No sign of anything, Joe?" Ned asked.

"Not yet, Ned. But don't worry, she'll be found. It was nice and warm all night, and it looks as if it's going to be a hot day. She'll be OK."

"You haven't been out all night, have you?" Ned asked.

"It's easier to hear things in the night," Old Joe said. "I thought I might hear her if she cried, but she was probably asleep. I dare say we'll find her today."

"I hope you're right," Ned said, "but I have to tell you, I'm beginning to wonder."

"About what?"

"About everything, Joe. The child is only two years old and we can't find a trace of her."

"Don't start making things worse in your head than they are on the ground," Old Joe said. "That's a bad habit we tend to get into." He laid his hand on Ned's shoulder. "Let's just size this up for a minute. We know she didn't drown in the river."

"I hope you're right," Ned said.

"I am right," Old Joe said. "The tide was out and we searched every inch of it. If she drowned we would've found her body right away. It never happened, I'll guarantee you that much."

"So, if she's not in the river then where is she?" Ned asked.

Old Joe didn't reply right away. He faced the river, but Ned could see his eyes were not focused on the water. He was deep in thought, drawing from events and crises long past.

"You have to remember two things, Ned," he finally said. "She is out here somewhere and we can never give up. This can only end when we bring the child home. Please God, she'll be alive when we do; but either way, we don't stop until she's home."

"Is there anything else I can do?" Ned asked.

"No, and don't be beating yourself up about it, either," Old Joe said. "Ned, if this was someone else's child would you be doing anything different?"

"No, I don't suppose I would," Ned said.

"Then why do you expect more from yourself? You're doing everything you can to help with the search, and you're doing it right. Just keep it up."

It was just then, before Ned could thank his mentor for his reassurances, they were interrupted by the commotion of the bolting animals.

"Now what's going on?" Ned asked Joe.

"I don't know and I don't care," Old Joe said. "Maybe the devil himself has come up for a visit, but unless he's going to lend a hand, he's going to have to wait to be seen. Finding Penney is the only thing that's important. Make sure all hands understand this."

"You're right," Ned said. "I'm going to see where everyone has been, and find out where else we need to look. I expect more men will show up today, so we should be able to cover a lot more ground."

"Don't worry, my son," Old Joe said. "We'll find her. Just keep everyone searching until we do."

"You should rest for a while before you go anywhere else, Joe. Lucy is probably getting worried about you."

"Lucy gave up worrying about me forty years ago," Old Joe said. "I'm fine, but I am going to make a quick run up to the house to put on some dry socks. Then I'm going to work my way across the marshes to Black Duck Pond, so don't send anybody else in there."

"Joe, I appreciate that," Ned said.

"Just keep the faith, young fellow. Just keep the faith," said Old Joe, and with a final reassuring pat on his friend's shoulder he turned towards his own little house.

Ned watched the tough old man climb over the fence to get out of the meadow.

"Friends are better than gold any day of the week," Ned thought. "Especially when they're made of iron."

After frightening the animals, the crunnocks reassembled in the woods not far from where Ned and Old Joe had just met. They were all relishing in the bit of mischief they had just indulged in.

"That was perfect, Sor. It was a great idea."

"Did everyone find something to chase?" Sor asked.

"Yeah, I did."

"Me, too."

"We chased a whole stable full of sheep. It was the most fun we had in ages. When can we do it again?"

"We'll find something even better to do later," Sor said. "Don't worry; I have lots of great ideas."

"Sor, what about the girl and Ral?" Drog asked. "Do you want me to take you to them now?"

"Oh yeah, I forgot all about them," Sor said. "I suppose we better get going. I did promise you I would go see what you had, didn't I?"

"It's not much farther," Drog said. "It's going to be more fun than what we just had."

"I doubt it, but we'll see," Sor said. "Come on everyone. Let's get moving so we can see what Drog and Ral have for us."

He allowed Drog to lead them into the woods again. He could have kept the crunnocks in Pinchgut a while longer to get the people stirred up again, but he reasoned it could wait until later. As long as they had Penney, the people would be easy picking.

"We're almost there," Drog said to Sor every few minutes. Finally, they reached the thick woods where he left Ral and Penney. "They're right in there."

With Sor and Drog leading the way, the crunnocks surged into the thicket. Right before their expectant eyes there was—nothing.

"What kind of a trick are you trying to pull?" Sor roared. "I'll thrash you until every bit of you hurts!"

"But, Sor, I swear they were here," Drog said. "This is where I left the two of them. Something must have happened."

"We better find them or this will be a sorry day for you," Sor said.

Some of the crunnocks began to poke around through the woods to see if there was any sign of Ral. After a couple of minutes one of them cried out. His name was Lirap.

"Look at what I found."

"Bring it here," Sor said. It was Ral's club.

"See, I told you he was here," Drog said, with a huge smile. "The girl was here, too. Just like I told you."

"It's touching to see your concern for our friend," Sor said. He looked at the club. "That idiot doesn't own anything except this. He'd never leave it."

"You think the young one did something to him?" Lirap said.

"I doubt it," Sor said. "They're not much good for doing anything when they're young. Something is not making sense here."

"Maybe Drog is making the story up," Lirap said.

"No, I don't think so," Sor said. "Judging by the way the people are searching, somebody took something from them. It has to be one of their young ones to have them in such a panic."

"Where is she then?" Lirap questioned.

"Good question," Sor said. "We don't have her and they certainly don't—and where's Ral? Let's go back to where they're all looking for her and see if we can get this figured out."

As the crunnocks left they passed by an old rampike. The rampike was once a black spruce tree, but life had long since departed from it. It was now a grey skeleton of its former self, full of knotholes, stubs of limbs—and two starrigans. Unbeknownst to Sor, he and the crunnocks were being carefully watched by the two Starrigans that Krab and the others left there the previous evening. They spent the night concealed under curtains of moldow, about halfway up the old tree. Having heard everything that was said they came out of their hiding place. Knowing Krab planned to head for Island Pond River they decided one of them would go to him, and the other would bring their information to Savid in Little Brook Bottom.

Island Pond River is very pretty and very small. It is hardly even worthy of being called a river. It's really just a brook, but a very nice brook that meanders between Island Pond and the Rocky River valley. In the dry middle of the summer the water is only deep enough to reach halfway to a child's knees; yet, the soft trickle is deceptive. Flowing since the beginning of time, the water has worn the sharp edges from the black rocks on the riverbed, leaving them round and smooth. The bright sun, beaming down on the dark rocks, warms the water nicely. It is an idyllic place and Penney enjoyed being there. She was also enjoying her friendly playmates. Soc was her favourite, but since the rescue, she had grown quite fond of all of them. Now, at midmorning, she was sitting on the soft moss with her toes in the warm water eating sweet, juicy bakeapple berries. She loved the tangy taste, and the bright red and yellow colours of the wild fruit.

"She seems to be happy so far," Krab said.

"She's fine," Soc said. "Do you think she's safe here?"

"I don't know. I hope so. I wish I could talk to Savid right now."

"What do you think she'll do?"

"She won't do anything until she knows more about the crunnocks," Krab said. "She'll want to know where they are. What they're up to. She'll want to know just what we're up against before she does anything."

One of the starrigans who was standing look-out spotted someone coming across the barrens towards them.

"Someone's coming," he yelled.

"How many?" Krab asked. The starrigans were alert.

"Only one," called the look-out. "It's one of ours."

The starrigans relaxed again. The newcomer was one of the spies they had left in the rampike. The look-out beckoned for the spy to join them, and in a few seconds she was in the clearing with them. After taking a few minutes to catch her breath, she began to tell her story as the starrigans gathered around.

"What did you find out?" Krab asked.

"Plenty," the spy said. She relayed the information she had regarding numbers, weapons and so on.

"This is perfect," Krab said. "Even though we have Penney and captured one of them, they have no idea we even exist. We have to use this to our advantage."

Shortly after the first spy delivered her intelligence to the rescuers at Island Pond River, her companion reached the cross-paths on the way to Little Brook Bottom. Out of earshot from Ral he was able to confer with Mot and Nak and confirm for them what Mot had been able to put together by interrogating Ral. Mot then dispatched him to Little Brook Bottom to deliver the same information to Savid.

She had retreated to her burrow the night before, shortly after Drek brought the dramatic news about the appearance of the crunnocks and the planned attempt to rescue Penney. She only came out for a short while when Nuf arrived from Island Pond River with the good news that the little girl was secure for the time being. The night had not been wasted, though. She spent it considering the challenges that presented themselves in the last day. The starrigan clan was distressed by the crunnocks' arrival and needed reassurance it was not the end of their world. Mot was holding one of them prisoner. What should they do with him? Looming above it all, however, was the immediate and much more urgent problem of how to get Penney safely home.

It was well after dawn when Savid reappeared from her burrow. She still needed more information about the crunnocks in order to make a sound decision. A little later in the morning the information was provided when the spy who had spent the night in the rampike arrived in Little Brook Bottom via the cross-paths. All the starrigans gathered around Savid while the spy gave his report.

"There are about a hundred of them." Worried glances passed among the starrigans. "They're a rowdy bunch. Their leader is called Sor. He bullies the others."

"Where are they now?" Savid asked.

"They went back towards Pinchgut to see if they could find Ral and Penney."

"Savid, what are we going to do?" the starrigans asked.

"First things first," Savid said. "We have to understand the most important thing now is the little girl. Her safety depends on us."

"But what about the crunnocks?" the others said.

"We have to find ways around them," Savid said. "We have to do whatever is necessary to get the child home, regardless of the cost. You must understand that." She saw them nod in agreement. "We have to accept the crunnocks may be here to stay."

"What about the crunnock Mot and Nak have with them?" asked the spy.

"We will deal with him when Penney is back with her parents. Right now, we need to keep watching the crunnocks." She looked around the group. "I need two volunteers to go to Pinchgut."

"I'll go," one called Gable said.

"Count me in," Laup said.

"Stay out of sight," Savid said. "Report back here at dark tonight—earlier if anything important happens." She then called Drek to her side. "Go to Island Pond River and tell Krab to come here to me. On your way along, tell Mot to keep the crunnock at the cross-paths and out of sight."

"Is there anything you want me to tell Soc and the others?" Drek asked. "They're going to want to know what we're doing."

"Tell them we're going to find a way to get Penney past the crunnocks. She can't be kept outdoors. It won't stay warm and dry for long and human children need shelter." She also gave Drek a small packet. "Take this with you. Mix it with a little water and rub it on the child. It will protect her from the bites of flies and nippers."

Chapter 7 - Jenny

Jenny turned away from the window and sat at the kitchen table. A moment later she got up and paced around the room. Then she went back to the window. It was the same pattern over and over again. She saw nothing when she looked out the window. She ate nothing when she sat at the table, and her constant pacing took her nowhere. She had no tears left to cry. She listened only for one voice and, until she could hear it and reply to it, she had nothing to say.

Sues Duggan and Lucy O'Reilly kept a close vigil over her. One or both of them had been at her side since the crisis started, and they would stay until it was over, but their dilemma was they could do nothing to comfort the young mother.

Once again, Jenny went over the previous day in her mind. Michael was up and dressed for work before the blast of the mill's steam whistle woke Penney at six-thirty. They joined him in the kitchen, and he fed Penney toast that he dunked in tea. Jenny protested the little girl was too young to be allowed tea, but it was just as well if she complained to the stove. Penney loved the sweet tea and toast, and one of Michael's greatest joys was to have her face and hands dripping wet when she gave him a sloppy hug and kiss before he went to work each day. Then Penney stood on a chair so that she could see him through the kitchen window. She didn't take her eyes off him while he walked across the bridge and entered the millyard. He always waited outside until the whistle blew again at five minutes before seven, signalling the workers to stand clear of the saws, while the mill started. The last thing he did every morning, before stepping inside the mill, was wave to her. She was always waiting in the window across the river to wave back.

After Michael went to work Jenny's routine was the same as it had been on hundreds of other days. Penney had to be bathed and dressed. It was a fine day so Jenny dressed her in a little brown dress that was suitable for wearing outdoors. Knowing Penney's propensity for getting into a mess, she put an apron over the dress, thinking it might save at least one change of clothes later. Water had to be boiled to wash the breakfast dishes and, while she washed the dishes, more water was heating to wash the laundry. All morning she scrubbed clothes on a washboard in a tub and hung them outside on the clothesline to dry. Penney completely changed Jenny's feelings about wash days. Scrubbing clothes was hard work and a task Jenny once loathed, but since Penney came along it was fun. The little girl loved to get her hands and arms down into the big soapy bubbles and was constantly soaking wet. Jenny enjoyed it almost as much as her daughter. About eleven-thirty Jenny put her iron frying pan on the stove and began to render out some fatback pork. Michael caught a half-dozen trout under the bridge the previous evening and she had promised him, as long as he cleaned them, she would cook them for his lunch. She rolled the trout in flour and placed them in the frying pan, cooking them until they were nice and crisp. She had just laid the trout on a plate with a couple of slices of bread she baked the day before, when the noon whistle sounded at the mill. Penney danced and clapped her hands when she heard the whistle.

"Daddy, Daddy," she squealed. Running to the window, she watched him retrace his steps to home until he could scoop her up in his arms again. She always sat either next to Michael or in his arms while he ate his lunch. She pestered him to share his trout with her, and fussed while her mom checked to make sure Michael had removed all the bones. When she finally got some trout, Michael roared with laughter as she screwed up her face at the taste of the mustard he had smeared on it. After lunch Penney gave her dad more hugs and kisses before he headed back to work. Then she waited in the window to wave at him again as he went back inside the mill when the stand-clear whistle blew at five to one. Jenny cleaned up the lunch dishes and went back to washing the laundry. Penney followed her around the house and out to the clothesline. She played about the yard while Jenny went back and forth with the clothes. It was a perfectly normal day in every way—until the unthinkable happened.

No matter how often Jenny went over every minute of the previous day, she could not come up with anything to explain Penney's disappearance. The little girl was in the yard playing when she went inside to get the last of the laundry. She wrung the water out of a couple of shirts and went back outside. Penney was gone. She was never away from her daughter for more than three or four minutes, and the door was left open the whole time.

"This can't be happening," she thought. "I'm going to wake up and Penney will be here." But it *was* happening. The nightmare was real and her little girl was still gone.

Jenny was fast becoming a victim herself. She was the youngest of nine children and was only four years old when her own mother died on the tail end of one miserable winter. Other than some foggy recollections of a kind voice and a warm lap, Jenny could hardly remember her at all. Even by

Pinchgut's meagre standards her family was never well-to-do. Her mother's death shifted them even farther away from prosperity. Her father, Johnny Dwyer, was a nice enough fellow who tried hard, but never could get seven days food into the house in seven days. His misfortunes were legendary. If he didn't lose his axe altogether, he broke the handle. If one horse in the place was lame, it lived in Johnny's stable. Every potato bed in Pinchgut might produce barrels of fine round potatoes in the fall of the year, but Johnny's would be cursed with canker. Rabbits chewed their way out of his snares before he got to them. The fat salmon that found their way to his nets were feasted on by hungry dogfish. Jenny was only twelve when he too, passed away. The only thing he left her was a steely determination not to live the hand-to-mouth existence of her youth for the rest of her life.

She also inherited, from her mother everyone would agree, stunning good looks that blossomed as she progressed through her teens. Her father told her one time, people treat you the same way you treat them, and the advice stuck. She worked hard to be pleasant and helpful. It paid off when she became old enough to be courted.

Every young man for miles around wanted to be seen with her, but again, her good sense prevailed. She considered and declined all of their offers with grace. She didn't burn bridges or end friendships, but none of the suitors was the one with whom she wanted to spend her life. Then one evening, about a month before the parish garden party, Michael caught up with her walking on the bridge. He managed, after great effort and with much blushing, to ask her if he could walk her home after the garden party dance. She had known Michael and his family since she was a child. He was a really nice fellow, who was well liked by everybody and, as the young ladies in the place would agree, was more than a little handsome himself. Added to this, he was Ned Duggan's son, and Ned had taught his sons how to work. Their families would be well provided for. Still, he was speechless when she accepted his advance. For her part, she never for a moment regretted her decision.

It would have been understandable if the challenges of her childhood had caused Jenny to be resentful and covetous about the prosperity of others—happily, this was not the case. Instead, Jenny was instilled with a sense of practicality. She believed, if you wanted something, the best way to get it was to plan and work for it. In similar fashion, she also believed when things went wrong, it was likely the result of neglect; the wisdom of which was dubious. Jenny was a careful and loving mother but, because of her way of thinking, she assumed the blame for her little girl's disappearance.

Why didn't she take Penney inside with her when she went in for more laundry?

Why didn't she stay out with her?

Why didn't she watch her daughter more closely?

Why was everyone trying to make her feel better?

Why was Father Quigley telling her to pray more?

Couldn't he understand that she had prayed every prayer she knew and nobody was answering?

Why can't they find Penney? She has to be out there somewhere. They need to look more. That's it. They're not looking everywhere. She would find Penney herself. She bolted for the door.

"Jenny! Wait. Where are you going?" Sues stopped her before she got outside.

"Let me go," Jenny said. "I have to find Penney. She's out there by herself and if no one else can find her, I will."

"Jenny, stay here," Sues said. "The men will find her. You can't go out there running through the woods." Sues put her arms around the distraught young mother, but Jenny was more than she could handle.

Lucy grabbed hold of her, too. Together they tried to bring the young woman to her senses. "Jenny my love, the men know what they are doing. Michael and Joe and Ned won't stop until they find her." She tried to stay between Jenny and the door. "They're out there now. They won't give up. They'll find her and bring her home to you."

"They can't find her," Jenny said. "I have to do it. Why can't you understand?" Sues and Lucy struggled to control the hysterical woman. "I have to find her before it gets dark again. I can't leave her out there for another night. Let me go."

"Listen to me, Jenny," Sues said. "I know you want to go out there, but you have to stay here for Penney. You must be here when they bring her home. She will want you."

That's right," Lucy said. "You have to wait here for her. You have to be here when she gets home."

Jenny nodded through her tears. She let her mother-in-law and Lucy lead her back to the table.

"Michael and the men will find Penney," Sues said. "They'll search everywhere until they find her. They won't ever give up."

"You can be sure of that," Lucy said. "They will find her and bring her back to you."

The older women were doing everything they could to comfort and reassure Jenny, but they had grave doubts about this ending well. The child had no way of feeding herself and must be hungry, but that wouldn't kill her. The warm dry weather wouldn't last long. Penney was soon going to be cold and wet, and this combination often brought down strong men. Both of them knew if Penney was going to be brought home alive, it had better happen soon.

Chapter 8 - Adversity Grows

The crunnocks followed Sor back to Pinchgut. At the edge of one of the meadows on the outskirts, Drog approached him.

"What do you want us to do now?" Drog asked Sor.

"I couldn't care less," Sor answered. "Am I supposed to hold your hand all the time?"

"Sorry," Drog said. "I just thought you might have plans for us."

"If I did, I'd tell you," Sor said. "Go do whatever you want to, but I want to see everybody over there, in the woods by the mill, right after dark."

"Those woods over there, by that mill?" Drog asked.

"Do you see another mill besides that one?" asked Sor. "Just get out of my sight. You already wasted enough of my time." As Drog turned to go Sor grabbed his arm. "Tell everybody to let me know right away if they see any sign of the girl or Ral."

"I'll come and get you right away," Drog said.

Four or five other crunnocks approached Sor and Drog. Sor could see they wanted to ask something.

"What is it now? What do you want?" he snapped.

"Oh, we didn't want you, Sor," one of them said. "We just wanted to ask Drog if he wanted to come with us for the day."

"What?" Drog asked. "I mean, yeah. Sure I'll go with you." Turning to Sor and raising his voice, he asked, "Do you need me anymore, Sor?"

"Not likely," Sor said. "Just don't do anything else to the people unless I know about it first. Make sure everyone understands this. Did you hear me?"

"I hear you, Sor," Drog said. "I'll tell them."

Sor watched Drog run off with the others. "He's their hero now, but when I figure out what's going on around here, I'm going to shove him so far down the rest of them won't remember what he looks like."

Once Drog was out of sight Sor climbed a tree at the edge of the meadow and scanned Pinchgut. People were scurrying everywhere. He noticed there were more men searching now than there were just a few hours earlier. He shook his head as he watched them.

"Where are they coming from? This is bigger than I figured."

Drek arrived at Island Pond River about mid-morning. Krab and the others gathered around him.

"Did Savid tell us what we should do?" Krab asked.

"Hang on, will you," Drek said. "I want to see Penney first."

"She's there by the brook, paddling her feet in the water," Krab said. "What did Savid say?"

Drek ran to the edge of the brook. Penney laughed when she saw him. Soc was sitting in Penney's lap. "Wow," Drek said. "She really is here. Did you have any trouble getting her to walk this far."

"It took a long time," Soc said. "The poor thing was exhausted."

"Drek, what did Savid say?" Krab asked.

"Oh yeah," Drek said. "She said for you to go back to Little Brook Bottom. I have to stay here and take your place."

"Did she say anything else? What are we going to do with Penney?"

"We have to keep her safe until we can get her home," Drek said. "She said no matter how hard we try, we can't take the place of her parents for very long."

"What did Mot and Nak do with the crunnock?" Krab asked.

"They only brought him as far as the cross-paths. Mot didn't want him to find out where we lived."

"Good thinking," Krab said. "What are they going to do with him?"

"Savid wants Mot and Nak to keep him there for now," Drek said. "Mot got the daylights frightened out of him. He got him convinced we're going to cook him."

"Good for Mot," Soc said. "I hope he scares the savage senseless, after what he did to Penney." She handed the little girl another juicy bakeapple berry. "I only hope we can find a way to get her home soon."

"We will, Soc," Krab said. "Savid will figure something out. Anyway, I'd better be moving. See you soon." Amid a chorus of goodbyes from his friends, he scooted through the trees and headed across the barrens to home. After he left, Drek sat down on the grass near Penney. He looked at Soc.

"How is she doing?"

"She's doing OK for now," Soc said. "She's warm and dry and she loves bakeapples, but she misses her parents. It's getting harder to keep her happy."

"Maybe we should try to find a way to keep her busy," Drek said, "so we can keep her mind off her parents."

"We have plenty of time," Soc said. "We won't be any worse off for trying."

By early afternoon Penney was getting restless, and Soc decided it was time to find a way to amuse Penney. She came up with the idea to hike along the side of the river so that it would look as if she was going home. It would also keep her busy, and hopefully tire her out, so that she would sleep well come nighttime.

It was a marvellous sight the birds and animals living at Island Pond River saw that day—a real parade along the riverbank. Drek in front, and Penney with the little starrigan, Soc in her arms next, followed by two more star-rigans. One stayed behind in case a messenger showed up from Little Brook Bottom. Penney laughed and clapped her hands in delight as the starrig-ans jumped and tumbled through the trees to amuse her. Every bird and butter-fly along the way became a participant in the parade. Young robins, just learning the mystery of flight, led the group through the alders to where the forest was a landscape of living Christmas trees. Brown rabbits, that could stand so still even hunters with the keenest eyes passed right by them, felt no threat from the party and joined right in. The rabbits allowed Penney to touch their silky soft fur and she giggled at their twitching noses while they showed the starrigans the safest and driest way to lead the child through the woods. Throughout the day, they stopped to gorge themselves on the bright red cracker-jack berries and to drink clear water from the river. Drek and the others soon realized that their problem might not be keeping Penney amused—it would be keeping her awake until they got back to their campsite. However, it worked out well, and they got her back just as the sun was disappearing for the day. The starrigan who had stayed in the camp had a big pile of bakeapple berries picked for Penney. But she was so tired she barely touched the berries before she rolled back into the warm dry grass and fell into the peaceful sleep of a much-loved and well-cared-for child.

Krab arrived back in Little Brook Bottom about midday. After he assured Savid and the others Penney was still secure, Savid took a minute to praise him for his clear thinking when he first encountered the crunnocks.

"You used your head," she said, "and because of it, the little girl is safe. Now, we will work together to get her home."

"What do you have in mind?" Krab asked.

"I see three different ways to go about it," Savid said. "We can try to bully our way right through the crunnocks. The problem with this approach is that a lot of starrigans and a lot of crunnocks might get hurt. So might Penney."

"I don't think we should try that," Krab said. "Besides, there are many people in the woods looking for Penney, and it'll do no good for them to see us or the crunnocks."

"That's true," Savid said. "The crunnocks still don't know anything about us, and I would just as soon keep it that way. So let's rule out the first option for now."

Krab said, "We can wait until the crunnocks move somewhere else or trick them into moving."

"Precisely," Savid said. "That was my second idea. You're still thinking."

"The problem," Krab said, "is we haven't got time to wait. The crunnocks could hang around for days. What's the third idea?"

"We will lead the searchers to Penney," Savid said.

"How can we do that?" Krab asked.

"We will leave clues for them. That way Penney will get to go home with her family and the crunnocks won't see us."

"What about the one Mot has?"

"Ah yes," Savid said. "I keep forgetting about him—and I'm going to continue to forget about him until later. I'm quite certain that will work out as well."

Krab laughed at Savid's simple approach to a difficult problem.

"I'll tell Mot to stay where he is when I get to the cross-paths again," Krab said. "I'm sure he's finding ways to keep himself amused."

"Tell him not to harm the crunnock," Savid said. "No good ever comes from hurting someone else."

"He won't do anything to hurt him," Krab said. "In the meantime, we need to put something belonging to Penney where the searchers will find it—we might be able to lead them to Island Pond River."

"We have to be sure the people find the clues, not the crunnocks," Savid said. "We don't want to lead them to Penney."

"You're right," Krab said. "It's not going to be easy, but I'm sure we'll come up with a way."

"You need to know something else," Savid said. "Tonight will still be warm and dry, but a terrible storm is on the way. It will be here by tomorrow evening. Krab, Penney needs to be home before it starts."

Krab accepted Savid's information as facts that didn't need to be questioned.

"Savid, you remember the night Penney was born?" he asked. "You gave me something to help Jenny. Is there anything you can do now?"

"No," she said. "It was only Jenny then. Now too many are involved. They are changing things by the minute." She raised her head and spoke to the sky. "It can't be controlled. It's up to us to do the best we can."

"I'll go back to Island Pond River," Krab said, "and try to find a way to lead the people to her."

"You do what needs to be done," Savid said. "Just be careful."

"Don't worry," Krab said. "She'll be home soon." He smiled and waved at her as he trotted out of the knoll.

He stopped when he reached the cross-paths to have a few words with Mot and Nak. A sullen Ral was sitting nearby.

"Any word on what I am supposed to do with this twit?" Mot asked.

"Savid says you're to sit tight for now," Krab said. "The cook will deal with him later when things settle down." He made sure to speak so that Ral could hear him.

The expression on the crunnock's face told Krab that he'd heard every word, but before they could say anything else, Mot spotted another starrigan coming towards them at top speed.

"Now what?" Mot asked as he beckoned to the newcomer to join them.

It was Laup, one of the two Savid sent to Pinchgut that morning. He was near exhaustion and collapsed at Mot's feet.

"The crunnocks got Gable," he gasped.

Krab and Mot were speechless. Nak helped Laup to his feet. It was the prisoner, Ral, who broke the silence.

"Looks as if things are getting even," Ral said. "I wouldn't plan a cook-up just yet."

A threatening glare from Mot silenced him.

"What happened?" Nak asked. "How did they get her?"

"We were careful, but they were everywhere," Laup said. "We were in the meadow by Penney's house and we could see them on the other side of the river around the mill. We decided to split up so that we could watch them better."

"That's when they got her?" Krab asked.

"She went up the river to cross to the other side, but some of them must have been up there and saw her. When she got near the mill a bunch of them were waiting for her."

"Wait until I get my hands on them," Mot said. "I'm going to beat them with their own arms."

"They grabbed her before she could get away and took her up in the woods. That's when I lost sight of her." Laup needed help to stay on his feet. "I was afraid to cross the river in case they might see me, too. Poor Gable. What will we do?"

Krab, Nak, and Mot looked at each other. This put a whole different twist on a situation that was already complicated.

"Go back and talk to Savid," Mot said.

Gable never saw them coming. She and Laup had been very careful as they travelled from Little Brook Bottom. They stayed away from the trails and open country, moving like two silent ghosts through the tangle of undergrowth. Caution rather than speed had been their creed all morning. She was especially careful crossing the river after she and Laup decided to split up. She went upstream, well beyond the farthest point where they had seen any crunnocks, and then crossed as fast as she could. Still, she thought, that's the only time they could've spotted her. They followed her back down the river where six or eight of them ambushed her near the mill.

Gable had a reputation among the starrigans for being willing to try anything once. Many considered her reckless, but she didn't see things that way at all. She simply felt confident in her own abilities. That was Savid's assessment of the little daredevil as well, and she didn't hesitate to give her the dangerous assignment of gathering intelligence in Pinchgut Gable managed to hide her initial reactions to being captured. She was angry at the crunnocks for ambushing her, and frustrated with herself for allowing it to happen. A degree of despair crept in with the realization that this was real life, and she was a real prisoner. She had no idea how the crunnocks would treat her, and the thought that she may never see Little Brook Bottom again wouldn't leave her mind. Notwithstanding all of that, she had developed her confidence over time by observing challenges, and finding ways to overcome them. Her analysis of the crunnocks started as soon as she was captured. She soon figured out it would be best for her to show no sign of fear or weakness as she was being led before the one who appeared to be their leader. She also came to the conclusion that, in spite of their bluster and the legends surrounding them, they weren't as fearsome as they would like to be; or as smart as they needed to be.

Sor was astounded. He couldn't believe his eyes. He had heard many legends about starrigans from the elders of his clan, but he'd never seen one or met anybody who had. Like most other crunnocks, he passed them off as myths created by storytellers to entertain others during the long nights. Yet, here in front of him, was a real live starrigan!

"My, oh my," Sor said. "What have we captured here?" He laid his hand on Gable's head, as if to make certain she was real.

"Take your filthy paw off me," she hissed.

"Oh, you are a feisty one, aren't you?" he said. "Well, at least you speak our language, although not as good as we do. What's your name?"

The defiant expression on Gable's face told him he needn't expect a response.

"How many of them were there?" Sor asked Lirap, who had led the capture.

"Just her, Sor," Lirap answered. "She crossed the river up past one of the islands and was heading this way. She was being real careful, as if she knew we were around."

Sor turned his attention back to Gable.

"I asked you, what is your name? Don't you know it?"

"Eat maggots," Gable said.

"Unusual name," Sor said. "But if that's what they call you, so be it." He swaggered back and forth in front of her. "How many starrigans are there? Where do you live? Do you starrigans have that girl and my clansman?"

"I'm not telling you anything," Gable said. "These fools jumped all over me and then dragged me here, and you expect me to talk to you?"

Sor stopped and stood toe to toe with Gable. He glared down at her.

"Little starrigan," he said, "understand this. Sooner or later you will be begging to tell me everything I want to know."

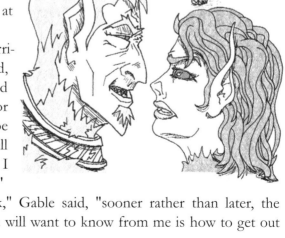

"Crunnock," Gable said, "sooner rather than later, the only thing you will want to know from me is how to get out of here."

"Tell me—where are the other starrigans?" Sor roared in Gable's face.

"What other starrigans?" she asked.

"Do you think I'm stupid enough to believe you're the only starrigan around here?" Sor said.

"I just met you," Gable said. "How am I supposed to know how stupid you are?"

Sor shook his club in the face of the defiant little starrigan.

"Be careful, starrigan. I have ways to make you talk."

"I didn't think even a crunnock would be stupid enough to make threats like that," Gable said.

"What are you talking about?" Sor asked.

"Tell me about this follower of yours who is missing. Is he bigger and stronger than me?"

"He could eat you for breakfast," Sor said.

"Really," Gable said. "Then tell me, great leader, how do you explain that he has disappeared, and the girl he is supposed to have captured is gone too?" She spoke up so that the other crunnocks could hear her. "Hasn't it crossed your mind that there might be powers at work here that you can't control? Don't threaten something you don't understand, because the time will come when you will have to account for yourself."

"I'm not afraid of any starrigan," Sor said. He knew the others had heard Gable's warning and he could see there was uneasiness spreading throughout the group.

Gable sensed the discontent of the crunnocks and pressed her advantage.

"There's no need to fear me," she said. But understand there is nobody involved in this search who is afraid of you.

And don't forget what I said earlier—the time will come when you will have to account for the actions of those you lead."

Sor tried hard to make sure the others didn't see he was confused and worried. For the first time in his life, he was faced with something he neither understood, nor was sure he could control. The legends he heard about starrigans always held them to be a timid breed, and inferior to the crunnocks. Yet this little starrigan showed no fear and, worse still, implied the starrigans had power that the crunnocks did not know about.

"I wish Ral and Drog had never come anywhere near this place," he said under his breath. He turned to the crunnocks holding Gable. "Put her out of sight. And don't hurt her. Keep her tied up but make sure she doesn't get away—we have to figure this out."

Savid was in her favourite seat on the root of the old witch-hazel tree when Krab and Laup tore back into Little Brook Bottom with the news of Gable's capture. Once again the starrigans descended into chaos. Savid, as always, remained calm. She took a few minutes to walk around to ponder the latest development. Then she stood in front of everyone and smiled.

"Well, that's one problem out of the way," she said.

"Savid," Krab said, "you make this sound like a good thing. It's not. It's terrible."

"You worry too much, my child," Savid said. "I'm not happy that Gable has been captured, but the fact is Penney is farther away from home because we didn't want to face the crunnocks. I, more than anyone, should have known better."

"What do you mean?"

"You have heard me say many times that everything happens for a reason. Crunnocks and starrigans have shared the world since time began. It will continue to be so. Now, we must use this change in circumstances to our advantage."

"I've never doubted you before, Savid," Krab said, "and I'm not going to start now, but I am worried about how this will turn out."

"Everything will be fine," Savid said. "That little girl belongs home with her parents, not out in the woods. The crunnocks don't understand the harm they might be doing to her or to themselves."

"I don't understand, either," Krab said.

"Human beings are strange," Savid said. "They've seen us from time to time." She smiled at Krab. "They know we exist, but they don't know, or care, that crunnocks and starrigans are different. We're all the same to them."

"How can we change their thinking?" Krab asked.

"We can't. What's important is that as long as they believe we won't hurt them they ignore us. When they think we might cause problems for them they will stop at nothing to get rid of us."

"You're going to do something," Krab said. "What is it?"

"It's time for us to take control so that we can resolve this dilemma," Savid said. "We need to talk to the crunnocks. Krab, go to the cross-paths and tell Mot to bring—what's his name? Ral? Yes, that's it. Tell Mot to bring Ral here to me. It's time to start talking."

As darkness settled over Pinchgut for the second time since Penney disappeared, Father Quigley was busy drying dishes in the schoolhouse up on the hill. Throughout the day dozens of searchers came through, all wanting the same things—the latest news and a quick lunch. A half-dozen of them had come in a while earlier and were sitting at the long wooden table. Their sweat-soaked shirts and the bog that stained their pants to the waist showed the difficulty of the terrain they covered. They had been in the woods searching since daylight. Now, sixteen hours later, they were wolfing down soup and sandwiches. A couple of the Pinchgut women hovered over them, pressing more food on them.

"Have more soup, young man."

"Thank you, ma'am. It's good."

"Have another sandwich."

"Thanks, but I've had plenty."

"Can I get you anything else?"

"Not now, ma'am, thanks. I just need to rest a bit before I go out again."

Father Quigley finished drying the last of the dishes and poured himself a mug of tea. He took the tea and a couple of raisin buns, and joined the searchers at their table.

"What do you fellows make of the situation?" he asked.

"I don't know, Father," the one nearest to him answered. "It's the strangest thing I've ever come across in my life."

"It's that for sure," Father Quigley said.

"I can't figure out why we can't find a single trace of her," one of his companions said. "It doesn't make sense to have this many men looking, and not one of us has been able to find as much as a track."

"Is she too small to leave a track?" the priest asked.

"She's bigger than most animals, Father," another said. "The best hunters for miles around are out there searching.

They can find something to shoot in the worst of years, but they can't find a trace of her."

"Well, Father," the first one said, "we don't want to be ignorant, leaving you here to eat by yourself, but we have to get back to the search."

"You fellows carry on," Father Quigley said. "Don't let me delay you. Leave those cups and plates. I'll clean them."

"Thanks, Father. Say a prayer for us and for her," one of them said as they walked to the door.

"My sons," Father Quigley said, "I haven't stopped praying since this started. The angels and saints are with you." He had to force himself to say the words. Prayers and novenas never known to fail had done so in the last two days. The lack of progress appeared almost sinister. It was as if a dark force was at work in Pinchgut.

"Get your head straightened out," he thought. "Your people need you." Once again he said a simple little prayer to St. Anthony, the patron saint of lost things. It was a mantra repeated a thousand times throughout the day in Pinchgut.

Dear St. Anthony, come around,
Something's lost and can't be found.

He finished his tea and began to clean the blackboard. Ned planned to get all hands together for a few minutes at ten o'clock if the child hadn't turned up by then. It looked as if the meeting would be going ahead.

By ten o'clock the schoolhouse was blocked with searchers. They stood around buckets filled with cold water, and were gulping it down by the dipperful as they shared information and theories. Ned stood in front of them.

Michael didn't attend. He opted to spend a few minutes with Jenny instead. Father Quigley led off with a prayer and then Ned reviewed what had happened and what areas had been searched so far. He was comfortable that everywhere in Pinchgut had been thoroughly searched, and a detailed search of every area within two miles was well underway.

"I know this for certain," Ned said to the assembly. "At least one place hasn't been searched—the place where she is. I don't believe a little girl can disappear into thin air anymore than a horse can."

"Please God, we'll have better luck tomorrow," a voice from the crowd said.

"I don't believe in luck, good or bad," Ned said. "There's an explanation for this. We just have to get to the bottom of it."

"You know we're with you," another voice said. "What do you want us to do?"

"We've searched the river up past the Crow's Nest," Ned said. "And we've been up the slide paths to Billy-Boy Pond. I think we should move to the northeast towards Island Pond at first light."

"Ned, I'm wondering if we're going the wrong way," said a deep voice from the back of the hall. It was Old Joe. Ned hadn't had a chance to speak to him since their chat in the meadow earlier that morning.

"What do you mean, Joe?" Ned asked.

"I've been going over it in my head," Old Joe said. "Remember how her cap was down in the river? Well, yesterday the wind was blowing in from the salt water. If the wind took her cap it would have blown it towards the woods, not the river." There was a murmur of agreement throughout the room. "If the cap was in the river she must have been down there too. You know how you were saying she always watched her father go back to work? Well, I wonder did she cross the river to follow him?"

"She could have, I suppose," Ned said.

"The water was low and she was used to seeing the boys out in the river at the logs," Old Joe said. "I'm thinking she could be in the woods on the other side of the river. It would've taken her only a few minutes to get across the river, and Jenny may have been inside the house a bit longer than she thought."

All around the room the men were talking to each other. Ned could see they were agreeing with Old Joe's theory.

"Wouldn't the fellows working in the millyard have seen her?" someone asked.

"Not necessarily," Edmund said. "There was only a few of us working outside and the place was going mad. We hardly had time to look up. An elephant could've crossed the river yesterday without us seeing it."

"Joe, we should've thought of that before," Ned said. "It makes sense. My God, don't tell me we've been looking in the wrong area all this time."

"It'd explain why we can't find any sign of her," Old Joe said. "In any case, we've searched everywhere as far as Billy-Boy Pond and there's nothing beyond that except open marsh and barrens until you get to Island Pond River. I can't see how any little child could get that far unless she was led there."

"True enough," Ned said.

"I think, first thing in the morning, we should start on the other side of the river," Old Joe said. "Search everywhere from here up to the Salmon Hole Marsh and down to the

Island Barasway." He turned to look at the men. "There are enough of us to do it in a day. If anybody finds a sign of her, come and get the rest of us, and we'll search together. By the way, bring your dogs. We should have been using more of them today."

"Do you want any of us to stay on this side?" another voice asked.

"We've gone over every area on this side a dozen times," Ned said. "No, I think it's best to put everyone in the woods across the river so that we can get the area searched before tomorrow night. We'll have the women and young children continue to look over here." He put on his cap. "Everyone go home and get a few hours sleep. Be in the millyard before daylight so that we are ready to start searching at daybreak. Father, how about a prayer before we go?"

Before Father Quigley could say anything someone in the back of the crowd spoke up.

"I think we should send for the constables," a woman said.

It was Alice Lastnor, the same woman who questioned Jenny's care for Penney earlier in the day. She had been in the schoolhouse since the search started. She was a tall thin woman who balanced a pair of wire-rimmed glasses on a sharp nose that constantly appeared in the middle of other people's affairs. She considered herself to be a courageous soul who spoke her mind, but just about everyone else considered her a meddling nuisance who rarely had a good thing to say about anything or anyone.

"Alice, just how do you figure that will help?" Ned asked.

"Well, I think there might be something more to this. A child just doesn't disappear."

"What exactly are you saying—that someone made off with the child?" Ned asked.

"I don't know and neither do you," Alice said. "But it seems strange to me that the child vanished the first time that she was left alone. I have my doubts about this whole affair."

"Alice," Ned said, "if you want to call in the constables go right ahead, but you look after them when they get here and keep them out of our way." The men were standing by then, sending a clear signal that they agreed with Ned. "We need these men for the search. We're not going looking after someone who doesn't know what they're doing."

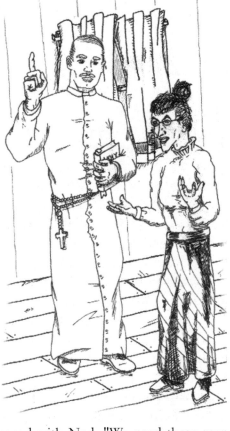

Thomas, Michael's older brother, wasn't so diplomatic. He stopped in front of the poker-faced women. "Alice, you're an old battleaxe. When this is over I'm going to rub your beak in whatever trouble you stir up." Ned stepped between Thomas and Alice, but Thomas kept talking. "You do whatever you like, missus. But I'm telling you to watch what you're saying. If Michael was here tonight, Father Quigley would be burying you tomorrow and we'd all be better off for it."

"Dear Lord," the priest said. "Let's not quarrel among ourselves. We have a far greater challenge before us and we must work together."

"Amen to that, Father," said Old Joe. "That's the best prayer I've heard from you in a long time."

The meeting ended on that note, but Father Quigley was disturbed by the discord he had witnessed. In his own mind, he knew Alice was wrong and Thomas did the right thing by confronting her. Still, seeds of ill will were in place and wouldn't go away. He knew if something positive didn't happen soon those seeds could grow into something ugly.

Ned was determined to stay focused on the search, and resolved to put Alice and her ilk out of his mind, and he said as much to Thomas on the way to their own houses.

"Thomas, remember, what goes around, comes around," Ned said. "Forget about her and her kind for now, but you can mark my words: the day will come when she will need help and she'll have to watch someone complaining in her face instead of lending a hand."

Old Joe forgot Alice as soon as she stopped talking. His mind was already on the woods and barrens across the river. "Where would I go if I was two years old?" he wondered, as he headed towards his own house for a short rest.

In the woods across the river from the schoolhouse, unseen in the darkness, Sor sat on a stump. He silently watched the people leave the meeting and go towards their houses. It would have pleased him tremendously if he had known about the malice that had raised its head within the community.

"Are they giving up?" asked Lirap, joining him.

"I doubt it," Sor said. "Most likely they will be at it again in the morning." Then he added with a grin, "Maybe we'll be able to find another way to make things interesting for them."

Mot was puzzled by Savid's command to bring Ral into Little Brook Bottom, but Krab assured him the instructions were clear. Ral, for his part, would have preferred to decline the invitation. He was not looking forward to meeting the leader of the starrigans. He couldn't help but notice the speed and alacrity with which the starrigans moved when their leader wanted something done. The crunnocks never obeyed Sor with such expediency unless they were in his line of sight. Their leader, Savid, must be a mighty warrior indeed to command such loyalty. He didn't feel any better when Mot warned him he would deal with any disrespect shown to Savid most severely.

It was after dark when Mot and Nak brought Ral to the starrigans' home. Ral noted, as he was led into the well-hidden knoll, that the starrigans had made a comfortable habitat for themselves. It was clean and tidy and looked much more welcoming than the hovels that Sor found for the crunnocks. The number of starrigans also surprised him. He had only seen two or three of them at a time and less than a dozen in total, yet he could tell at a glance that there were at least as many of them as there were crunnocks.

"If Savid has them all trained to fight like Mot, the crunnocks have something to worry about," he thought.

They were now in what appeared to be the centre of the community, but he still couldn't see anybody that looked like a leader. Just about all of the starrigans kept their distance and didn't speak. One ancient and shrivelled creature walked up to him and looked closely at him. Then she walked behind him. She seemed to take special note of his bindings. Without saying anything she walked away and went into a burrow. He was still looking around for the leader when the ancient one came back with a small vial in her hand.

"Untie him," she said to Mot.

"Are you sure, Savid?" Mot asked. "He may try to escape."

"He won't try to escape," she said. "He doesn't have to. He's free to go if he wants to."

Mot did as Savid instructed and untied the belt holding Ral. The crunnock couldn't make a run for it even if he wanted to. He was so shocked his feet wouldn't move.

"This was the mighty leader of the starrigans?" he thought.

"Your arms are sore," she said, looking at where the bindings had been. "This will help." She mixed a little of the powder from the vial with some clean water and rubbed it on his arms. He felt a strange tingling, followed almost immediately by relief. He was bewildered by the kindness and confidence displayed by Savid.

"Come, my child," Savid said. "Sit here with me. Don't be afraid. You're with friends."

Ral did as he was told and sat on the smooth log next to the ancient starrigan. She showed no fear and he realized, as well, he was no longer afraid.

"I'm sorry we did not treat you as well as a visitor should be treated," Savid said, "but the events of the last day have thrown us off a little bit. We need to talk, but before we do, you must eat. I understand you've eaten very little since you came into our company."

Savid motioned to a couple of starrigans standing nearby. They brought two large wooden bowls to Ral. One was filled with ripe juicy raspberries and bakeapple berries. The other held an assortment of delicious seeds. A bowl of clear water was also placed before the crunnock.

"Eat this to get your strength back," Savid said.

Ral had eaten little in the last two days, but he was still suspicious about this unexpected hospitality. Seeing Ral hesitate, Savid took some food from each bowl and ate it.

"It's delicious," she said. "Go ahead, try it."

Ral tried a little at first, and found it tasted just as good as Savid said it did. He began to gorge himself. In a very short time both bowls were empty and he washed the food down with cool, clear water. Savid smiled at him.

"That's better," she said. "Are you feeling stronger now?"

Ral nodded.

"You look strong and healthy," Savid said. "You must be well cared for. Have you always been a member of Sor's clan?" She spoke as if she knew the crunnock leader well and making casual small talk about his clan was an everyday occurrence.

"Yes," Ral said.

"Well," Savid said, "you must miss him and your friends. Please understand, you are free to go back to them whenever you want. Mot will show you the way if you're not sure how to get there."

"Why are you letting me go after what I did?" he asked.

"What you did was wrong," Savid said. "But keeping you against your will is also wrong. What did you expect to happen when Mot brought you here this evening?" Savid said.

"I thought you were going to cook me."

"Cook you?" Savid's jaw dropped. "Where in the world did you get such an idea?"

All eyes turned toward Mot who had a rather satisfied grin on his face.

"Oh my, you poor thing," Savid shook her head. "The only thing that's going to be cooked around here are the nippers' eggs that a starrigan with a poor sense of humour is going to find for me."

The starrigans laughed heartily as Mot's grin was replaced by an expression of righteous indignation. Ral even managed to smile a little himself, partially from relief and partially with chagrin, realizing that Mot had succeeded in bluffing him for so long. As he laughed, he realized that he had never seen the crunnock clan laugh as easily as these starrigans.

Savid became serious again. "Do you think it's better that we are friends or should we have done something to get even with you?"

"I like this better," Ral said.

The old starrigan smiled at him. "I thought you would. I want to ask you about the little girl. Why did you take her?"

"We didn't plan to," Ral said. "We were just there looking around when she chased some birds into the woods. When she started to follow us, we thought it would be fun to play some shenanigans on the people. I guess we went a bit too far, didn't we?"

"Were you going to hurt her?" Savid asked.

"No," Ral said. "We were just going to hide her until we could show her to Sor. We figured the people would find her in no time." He looked at the faces of all of the starrigans. "We weren't going to hurt her. Is she all right?"

Savid answered softly and slowly. "She is for now, but she will soon die if she is not returned to her parents."

The starrigans let out a collective gasp. Ral jumped up, but found himself wobbling on shaky legs. Panic could be heard in his voice.

"Die?" he said. "No, we can't let that happen. We have to get her home."

Savid raised her hand to quiet everyone down. She beckoned to Ral to take a seat beside her again. He did so, but his agitation was plain to see.

"It doesn't have to be that way, but much has to be done to get her home," Savid said.

"There are enough starrigans to get her past the crunnocks," Ral said. "Sor can't stop all of you."

"Perhaps," Savid answered, "but what happens if we fail? Will Sor bring the child home?"

"I doubt it," Ral said. "He knows the starrigans are here now, so his only thought will be to fight you. The girl is only good to him if she can help him defeat you."

"We have to get Gable back, too," Savid said. "What do you think he's done to her?"

The starrigans could see the question about Gable caused Ral even more distress. He kept his eyes locked on the ground as he answered.

"You have good reason to be concerned about her," Ral said. "Sor is probably pretty angry because he can't find me or the girl. He'll try to get Gable to tell him where you are." He paused and bit his lip. "He can be nasty, especially if he thinks someone is afraid of him."

"The risk to the child and to Gable is far too great for us to use any kind of force to save them," Savid said. "In any case, fighting is Sor's way, not ours, and we will do this on our terms."

"I'll do anything I can to help," Ral said. "I'm really sorry."

Ral had never felt as good about himself as he did when Savid smiled and took his hand in hers. "Those, my child, are golden words that only the very strong can use with ease. I'm sure you can help make things right again."

Savid got to her feet. Ral stood up as well and she linked her arm into his. It was a cloudless night and the stars were twinkling overhead.

"Walk with me," Savid said. "I will tell you what must be done. The rest of you must rest. We have much work ahead of us."

The starrigans then witnessed a scene that they could not have even imagined hours earlier. The brawny crunnock walked arm in arm with the frail old starrigan out the path to the side of Little Brook. Once there, they sat down on a log by the side of the brook and talked for hours. In the middle of the night, long after all the other starrigans were asleep, they finished their conversation and stood up. Savid put her arms around Ral and gave him a huge hug. She went back to the knoll while he set out towards Pinchgut. A great deal had happened in the last two days yet, in spite of it, the thing foremost in Ral's mind had nothing to do with the crisis looming over them. The only thing he thought about as he moved through the darkness was the hug that Savid had just given him. It was the first one he had ever received.

Savid didn't go back into her burrow after Ral departed. She was restless and spent the remainder of the night sitting in the hollowed whorl of the witch hazel tree. She left her seat several times to pace slowly around the knoll. It would have been obvious, if any of the other starrigans were awake to see it, that her mind was

troubled and she was in deep thought. The approaching dawn painted the eastern sky scarlet red. Nak was the first of the starrigans to shake off sleep and come out to greet the day. He noticed the crimson sky right away and mentioned its significance to Savid.

"It looks like we're in for some nasty weather," he said.

"Indeed we are, my child. Indeed we are," Savid said.

Sor was asleep in some dry grass behind the trees nearest to the mill when Drog came along to wake him up.

"What do you want?" Sor said. "How come I can't get a few minutes sleep without having to do something for one of you?"

"I'm sorry, Sor, but Ral is back," Drog said. "He says he needs to talk to you."

Sor was on his feet immediately. "Where is he?"

"Over by the trees where we have the starrigan," Drog said.

Sor was already in a foul mood after being roused from his sleep. It didn't improve when he saw so many of the crunnocks gathered around Ral. He shoved three or four of them aside and grabbed Ral by the shoulder.

"Where've you been?" Sor asked. "Where's that girl you're supposed to have?"

Ral didn't expect Sor to greet him with kindness or concern, but he was still taken aback by his hostility.

"The starrigans caught me," Ral said. "They have the girl, but I don't know where they have her hidden. Their leader sent me here with a message for you."

"A message?" Sor asked. "What is it?"

Ral looked at the crunnocks staring back at him. Then he took a deep breath.

"She told me to tell you that, for the good of everyone, you must release the starrigan you are holding prisoner and leave here so that they can return the child to her parents."

"She said? The leader of the starrigans is a she?" Sor said. "I'm supposed to take orders from some female starrigan? Are you crazy?" He smirked. "What does this great leader of the starrigans look like? Is she a giant?"

"No," Ral said. "She's old and small, but I think you should listen to her. She's very wise."

"Wise, is she?" Sor said. "Well, I don't take orders from any females, especially female starrigans. What's this wise old starrigan going to do if I don't listen to her? Is she going to come here and hit me with her cane?"

The crunnocks all laughed—all except Ral.

"She said that you must do exactly as she tells you, or you will meet your fate tonight on the second island up in the river."

"Meet my fate? She's threatening me? I'm fixing this right now. We're not waiting until tonight." He grabbed Ral and pushed him towards the riverbank. "You take us to the starrigans and we'll see who meets their fate."

"That won't work, Sor," Ral said. "I don't know where they are now. She expected you to react this way, so she moved the starrigans away from where they had me. She told me to tell you that we can go there if we want, but the place will be empty." He stood in front of Sor again and spoke softly. "Sor, I've never met anyone like her before. She's old, but she's brave and wise. You should listen to her."

"I'll never listen to some old fool of a starrigan or a fool of a crunnock, either," Sor said. "She has you frightened out of your wits, but she doesn't scare me. We're going to meet these starrigans and find out what they're made of." He raised his voice to make sure all the crunnocks could hear him. "We'll be on that island tonight, but chances are they won't even show up."

The other crunnocks roared their approval. Ral listened to them bragging about what they would do when they met the starrigans. They would chase the starrigans from here just like the crunnocks chased them from everywhere else. It bothered him to know that a just few days ago he would have sounded as loud and angry as the rest of them. He decided to try one last time to reason with Sor. It was a long shot, but it might work.

"Sor, please listen to me," Ral said. "Tell me about the starrigan that you have captured. Has she shown any sign of weakness?"

"We have her right where we want her," Sor said, but the look on his face told Ral otherwise. "By this time tomorrow when her clan is destroyed, she won't be as stubborn as she is being now."

"Listen to me," Ral said. He stepped closer to Sor so that the others couldn't hear him. "She's a small female and she hasn't broken. Many of them are as big and strong as we are. They captured me and took the girl. They know this place and they're not afraid of us. Wouldn't it make more sense to slow things down until we know them better?"

"I don't care how big they are," Ral said, "or how many of them there are. There won't be as many by tomorrow. We're going to cut down on the starrigans around here. Right?"

The clan members roared their approval. Ral could see that reasoning with Sor was useless, so he walked away. Most of the other crunnocks remained gathered around Sor, feasting on the excitement of the coming brawl.

"They sound like a bunch of twillicks," Ral thought. It was no compliment to be compared to the noisy bird that squawked empty threats from the air when something ventured into its territory.

He made his way to where Gable was being held. She was tied securely to a tree and guarded by three of the toughest crunnocks in the clan. He looked her over, paying particular attention to the knots securing her. She appeared tired and resigned to whatever fate was to befall her, but she did not show any sign of fear.

"You've got her hands and feet tied pretty tight. She won't get away," he said to the crunnocks guarding her.

"She's not going anywhere," one of them said.

"Perfect," Ral said. "Has she been giving you any trouble?"

"Nothing we can't handle."

"Good."

Gable had shown little interest in Ral up to then and he was surprised when she spoke.

"So you're the lout that's responsible for this mess," she said. "How does it feel to be one of the biggest cowards in the world?"

"You're in a poor position to be judging me," Ral said. "What makes you think I'm a coward?"

"What else would I call someone who steals children?" Gable said. "The whole group of you are cowards. Why else would you need three overgrown idiots to guard me?"

One of the guards jumped up with his fist raised to strike her, but Ral stopped him.

"Wait," Ral said. "Sor doesn't want to hurt her, yet. You can count on her getting what she deserves in good time."

The guard sat down again and Ral turned his attention back to Gable.

"I've got something special planned for you," Ral said.

"Forgive me if I don't stay awake waiting for it," Gable said.

Ral appeared to ignore her. He turned his attention back to the crunnocks guarding her.

"Are you planning to keep her here?" he said.

"This is as good a place as any," one of them said. "Why do you ask?"

"No reason," Ral said. "I was just wondering what we are going to do with her."

"Sor has to make up his mind on that one," the guard said.

"True enough," Ral said, and then bidding the guards good night, he sauntered back to join the rest of the clan.

Chapter 9 - Daybreak

The normal population of Pinchgut included forty able-bodied men. More than five times that number assembled in the millyard before daylight on the morning of the third day of the search. Every community within twenty miles was well represented. Most of them had bunked out in haylofts. In the last hour they passed through the schoolhouse in a steady stream where they were given a hearty breakfast of bacon, beans, and tea. After breakfast, sandwiches and cold cuts were pressed into their hands to sustain them for another day in the woods. The significance of the red dawn sky wasn't lost on them.

"There's heavy weather on the way," one said to Ned.

Ned nodded. "We have to find her today. Whatever it takes we have to do it."

The plan was simple. Ned arranged the men in a single line that stretched more than a quarter of a mile. They would push inland from the starting point until they reached the open bog lands almost two miles from the millyard. The search line would then split, with half of the group swinging to the north and working back to the river, while the other half of them would turn to work the country, heading to the south. The process would be repeated until they had covered the area upriver as far as the Salmon Hole, and down along the shore until they reached the place called the Island Barasway. If any signs of the child were found—footprints, a piece of clothing, anything that could be identified as being hers—a messenger would go to the mill and blow the steam whistle. That would be the signal for the men to come together and concentrate their efforts.

The searchers also brought with them every dog they could find. Some were fine hunting dogs, but many were just the small, yapping, little mixed breeds referred to as "crackies." The logic of bringing them along on the search was because even the most useless canine was an inquisitive creature and would explore every nook and cranny it passed. As such, they would be valuable in the search.

As soon as the dawn grew bright enough to see everything on the ground the search line moved out of the millyard and into the woods. The dogs went ahead of the searchers and, almost immediately, a crescendo of barking erupted.

"There's something here!" the volunteers yelled to each other. "The dogs found something!"

The search line broke ranks and the men poured into the woods, chasing the baying dogs that were running madly in all directions. Alas, the dogs had indeed found something, but it wasn't the missing child. The clan of crunnocks was dozing in the woods while the men assembled in the millyard just a short distance away. Only the few assigned to watch over Gable were awake, and they paid little heed to the men. The sight of the humans looking into, under, and around everything was no longer a novelty to them. They were also aware that the searchers moved slowly, and it was an easy matter to stay out of their sight. They had not, however, counted on the dogs.

A small black and white crackie named Brandy was the first to reach the treeline and, almost immediately, he spotted one of the crunnocks. He went after it with the same enthusiasm that he would use to pursue a wayward cat. The alarmed crunnock took to the trees, barely escaping the canine teeth nipping at his behind. The entire pack picked up on the excitement of Brandy's barking and rushed into the woods— straight to where the crunnocks were sleeping. The drowsy crunnocks woke in panic and confusion. Sor tried to yell directions while, at the same time, trying to avoid becoming a snack for a water dog named Willie. Willie was a cur renowned throughout Pinchgut for two things—being the ugliest mongrel to ever accompany a hunter, and being able to find game when no other dog or human could. However, his step had slowed because he was well into the second half of his life, enabling Sor to reach the safety of a tree before Willie's teeth snagged him. The din of the barking dogs prevented any effective communication among the clan, leaving every crunnock for himself. They ran in all directions with the howling dogs on their heels.

The only creature unable to escape was Gable—she was still tied to a tree. When the dogs entered the area she managed to remain unnoticed by freezing into a statue, a tactic perfected by the rabbits she knew so well. The strategy worked. The dogs' attention was directed at the fleeing crunnocks, but she knew that wouldn't last long. They would be back as soon as the crunnocks got away. She could hear the searchers calling to them, and it would only be seconds before the men reached her location as well. She had no cover and had been trying for hours to escape from her bindings. It was impossible to avoid discovery. The little starrigan could feel herself being overtaken by panic.

The first men to reach the crunnocks' site were Michael's brothers, Edmund and Thomas. Gable was only a dozen paces from where they stood and in plain sight. She was terrified. They only had to look in her direction to see her.

"Follow me if you want to live," a voice whispered in her ear.

Her despair only increased when she saw it was the crunnock, Ral. He untied her and pulled her into the underbrush behind the tree. Thomas caught the movement out of the corner of his eye.

"What was that?" he said.

"Probably a rabbit or a rat that the dogs scared up," Edmund said. "What the hell are they chasing anyway? There's nothing here that I can see."

Ral held Gable's hand and pulled her through the thick underbrush. As soon as they were out of sight, he stopped. He saw the confusion and fear in her eyes.

"Savid sent me to get you," he said. "I'll explain later if we get out of this mess alive. Give me your arm." Gable was too shocked to question him. He took the cord she had been tied up with and wrapped it around his arm and hers. "There are crunnocks everywhere. If we meet one, I'll do the talking. Come on, let's go."

Side by side they ran out of the underbrush and along a path. Ral planned to head upriver until they were out of sight and then cross to the other side, but they had only taken a few steps when they stopped dead in their tracks. They were face to face with Willie, the veteran of a thousand hunts. The old dog knew from years of experience when the chase was likely to yield results and when it was futile. He had abandoned the pursuit of the crunnocks almost immediately. He was quite content to let the young crackies go running after prey that couldn't be caught.

Now it appeared that his good sense had been rewarded with these two little tidbits right in front of his face.

"What will we do?" whispered Gable. "Do you think we can frighten him?"

"I don't think he backs down very often," Ral said. "Get ready to run." He let go of the strap binding their arms. "Now!"

Gable dashed to the left, but as she did she heard Willie emit a tremendous howl of rage. She looked over her shoulder to see that, instead of running, Ral had launched himself upon Willie's face. He was tearing at the dog's ears and kicking his eyes, but Gable could see the dog was getting the advantage. Willie expected his prey to run and was startled when Ral attacked him. Nevertheless, he had spent a lifetime battling every kind of wild creature and hundreds of other dogs. He didn't plan to lose his first fight today. Gable saw that Willie would soon pry Ral off of his face and then the crunnock would be helpless. In the moments that passed since he untied her, she had been uncertain about Ral's motives, but there was no doubt about what was happening now. He was buying time for her to get away and paying for it with his life.

The boldness which Gable was renowned for returned and she rushed back to join the fray. Just as the dog managed to swat Ral to the ground she leapt on its back. Before the angry dog could bite the crunnock Gable sank her teeth deep into its tail. Willie howled in pain and surprise. He spun around, tossing the starrigan into the bushes. As he moved towards her, Ral got back to his feet and leapt on the dog's head once again. This time he secured a tight hold on Willie's ears and bit them repeatedly. The dog's fury was exceeded only by his agony as Gable jumped back on him and sank her teeth into his tail again and again. The dog soon had enough. Gable and Ral jumped off and landed side by side in the moss. Willie ran towards home.

They lay there for a minute trying to catch their breath. Finally Gable spoke.

"That was the bravest thing that I ever saw anybody doing. That dog could have eaten you alive."

"Savid didn't mention that part to me." Ral grinned at her. "You were pretty good yourself. We better get going though, before some of the crunnocks see us."

"If they heard that dog howling they would have gone the other way. Maybe he did us a favour," Gable said.

"Let's hope we're spared from any more favours like that," Ral said.

Both of them scurried along the paths that led up the side of the river. Gable's speculation regarding the crunnocks' reaction to the dog was right. The crunnocks that were nearby lit out in the other direction when they heard Willie howl. In a short while the little starrigan and her rescuer were far enough upriver to cross over to the other side. When they were safely out of sight in the thick forest they stopped to make sure they were not being pursued.

"Looks as if we made it," Ral said. "We should be all right now. Savid said she would leave someone at the cross-paths to let us know where to meet them. Let's go."

"Hang on," Gable said. "I don't understand what's going on. Why did you free me?"

"It was the right thing to do," Ral said. "Savid let me go, so I did the same for you."

"You still didn't have to release me. Savid didn't make you do that, you could have just stayed with your friends."

"Listen, I've done some pretty stupid things over the last few days," Ral said. "That little girl is out in the woods because of me, and you got captured because you were trying to help her. I had a long talk with Savid last night and she helped me to understand a lot of things." He looked back along their path for pursuers. "I have to try to make things right. I had to help you and I have to make sure the little girl gets back to her parents."

"Can we do it?" she asked.

"We have to," he said. "Come on, let's find the others."

They started out again and were soon at the cross-paths. Savid had assigned Laup to wait there and he was overjoyed to see Gable approaching with Ral. The last time he saw her was when he witnessed her being captured in Pinchgut. He ran across the barrens to meet them.

"Thank heaven it's you," Laup said. "I was afraid I'd never see you again. Are you all right?"

"I'm fine," Gable said. "Thanks to our friend here." She smiled at Ral. "Where is everybody?"

"Savid moved the whole clan out to the woods on the side of Island Pond," Laup said. "She wants to be closer to Pinchgut and Penney. I think she has something in mind to get her home today or tonight. Where are the crunnocks?"

"They're still in Pinchgut," Ral said. "They had a little trouble with some dogs this morning. It's a safe bet that by now they're looking for the both of us. We better get to Savid and see what's happening."

"I'll go with you," Laup said. "All the others are there now and there won't be anyone else coming here."

Sor was out of sorts with the world. It was mid-morning and several of the dogs were still sniffing around for crunnocks. His clan was spread out all over the place and he had his cronies trying to round them up. But it was Ral and the missing starrigan that had him really upset.

"Didn't anybody see them?" he shouted. He looked from one to another. The crunnocks wilted under his glare.

"Maybe the dogs got her," one said. He was one of the three that had been assigned to guard Gable.

"Maybe the dogs got her," Sor said. "Maybe they didn't. Maybe she just flew away like a little bird." He grabbed the guard and yelled in his face. "You don't know what happened to her because you were asleep when you were supposed to be watching her."

"Sor, we were awake," the guard said. "She was there when the dogs showed up. We didn't have time to untie her. The dogs must have gotten her."

"You fool," Sor said. "How come there's no blood? Where did the rope go that we had her tied up with? Did the dogs eat that, too?"

"The dogs didn't get them," said another crunnock, just joining the group. "At least not here. I saw Ral run off with her tied to his arm. They headed upriver."

"See, what did I tell you?" Sor said. "The lousy, miserable traitor is bringing her back to the old starrigan who messed with his mind."

"Maybe Ral still has her out in the woods and is trying to get away from the dogs," the new arrival said.

"Yeah, right," Sor said. "And maybe he untied her because he thought the dogs were too fat and shouldn't be eating so much. The dogs will get a meal when I get my hands on him. I'm going to feed him to them, piece by bloody piece."

"What do you want us to do now?" another asked.

"Stop being stupid would be a good start," Sor said. "A couple of you wait here for whoever is not back yet. The rest of you spread out and find Ral and that starrigan." He clenched his fists as he spoke. "When you find them, come get me. I'll be somewhere around that second island."

"When do you want the rest of us there?" Lirap said.

"By nightfall," Sor said. "We're going to show the starrigans who is in charge around here." He pushed his way out of the group. "Don't just stand there like fools. Get moving."

The crunnocks dashed off in different directions. Sor watched them go and then started up river, railing to the trees as he went.

"Idiots," he said. "I'm surrounded by fools and idiots and traitors. Bamboozled by some old hag of a starrigan." He grumbled as he walked. "They'll never amount to anything, no matter how hard I try. At least after tonight there won't be any more starrigans to deal with. I can promise them that much."

The woods are thick on the east side of Island Pond. The low hills rising from the water's edge are covered with a dense stand of spruce and fir that is impenetrable to all but the smallest of creatures. Savid began moving the starrigans there soon after Ral left Little Brook Bottom to deliver her message to Sor. The clan was now much closer to Pinchgut and, although only a few of the starrigans knew it, they were also very close to where Drek, Soc, and the others were caring for Penney. Savid decided early that it was safest for the little girl if as few as possible knew of her whereabouts.

One of the starrigans saw Ral, Gable, and Laup approaching and beckoned them into the woods. The clan was elated to see that Gable was safe and sound. All of them were flabbergasted when she told them about the heroic role that Ral played in her rescue, especially how he had attacked the hunting dog to save her. Any doubts they had about his character were replaced by awe at having someone so courageous in their midst. They would never again doubt that there was good to be found in a crunnock.

After Ral and Gable gave the group an account of their adventure, Savid took them aside. Krab and Mot joined them. Their interest now was in trying to determine what the crunnocks were most likely to be doing during the rest of the day and what precautions, if any, the starrigans should take. Ral was certain that Sor would want to direct every resource at his disposal towards capturing him and Gable but, considering the confusion wrought by the dogs, it might be some time before he would be able to do that, and by then his priorities may have changed.

"I told him you moved the starrigans away from Little Brook Bottom, so I doubt very much if he is going to go there," Ral said. "My best guess is that they will spend the day looking for us and then go to the second island this evening and wait for us."

"That makes sense," Savid said, "but it also presents a problem. I was hoping to move Penney closer to home today so she wouldn't have as far to walk in the dark tonight. We can't take any chances moving her now because the crunnocks will have eyes everywhere."

"Savid," Krab said, "what's going to happen tonight? Are we really going to meet the crunnocks on the island?"

"Why do you think we're going to meet the crunnocks?" she asked.

"You told Ral to tell them to meet us there, didn't you?" Krab asked.

"No, I didn't," Savid said. "Ral, did you give Sor the exact message I asked you to give him?"

"Word for word, just like you told me," Ral said.

"Did I say we were going to the second island?"

"No, you didn't," Ral said. "You told them they would meet their fate on the second island. I'm sure they assumed we would be there to fight them. That's what I thought, too."

"I can't help it if they assume the wrong thing," Savid said, "even if I did nudge them a little bit in that direction."

"So what is going to happen?" Krab asked.

"Our plan hasn't changed," Savid said. "We are going to do everything we can to get Penney home. That's what we set out to do and that's the plan we're sticking with."

"I don't understand," Krab said. "What about the crunnocks? If we don't show up they're not going to stay on the island by themselves." He could see the others were also puzzled. "They'll know we're trying to get Penney home and come looking for us. What if they find us?"

"Krab," Savid said, "how well do you remember the night Penney was born?"

"You know I'll never forget that night," Krab said.

"Remember I told you then there are powers at work in the world that we don't understand?"

"Yes," Krab said. "You said if it was meant for us to help, a way would present itself. It worked out for the best that night."

"It did," Savid said, "and if it is meant for us to help tonight, a way will present itself. Our job is to do what we can to have Penney ready. Powers greater than us will decide whether or not we succeed."

"I don't know, Savid," Krab said. "This seems risky to me. You're depending a lot on these special powers. We're not even sure they exist."

Savid scowled at her sceptics, but seeing doubt in their eyes, she decided to explain further.

"I assure you the powers that I speak of do exist. The proof is all around you if you would only open your eyes to see it. Foxes are good hunters, are they not?"

They nodded.

"One of the things they hunt is rabbits, but we know even the best fox has a difficult time catching a strong healthy rabbit. The rabbit uses its speed to get away, so the fox has to settle for the sick or the lame." She stood and looked across Island Pond. "Tell me, though, why the foxes don't go after the very young rabbits? They can certainly use their noses to find the burrows with the young rabbits in them."

"No fox is stupid enough to put its face down into a rabbit's burrow where the young ones live," Mot said. "The mother rabbit would claw it to pieces."

"That's right," Savid said. "Now we all know that no rabbit is a match for a fox. Yet, not even the strongest fox will face a mother rabbit protecting its young." She sat down and looked at each of them. Seeing they were listening intently, she went on. "The bond between a mother and her young is one of those powerful forces that I speak of. We don't understand it, but we know it exists. The crunnocks are tampering with it now, and nature has proven time and time again that it will defeat those who defy it. The crunnocks don't know it yet, but they are picking a fight with an opponent far more dangerous than us. We have to care for Penney and, if it is meant that she should go home, a way will be found."

"How will we know?" asked Gable.

"We will know, my child," Savid said. "Just as a beaver can look at a shallow pond and know where to build a dam, we will know."

"What should we do in the meantime?" Ral said.

"We have to make sure that Penney is ready," Savid said. "Krab, go to Drek. Tell him to have Penney ready to travel tonight. Tell him we are going to try to bring her home."

"Anything else?" Krab said.

"Be careful," Savid said. "There's no great rush. Just get there safe and unseen."

"I'll be careful," Krab said. "I'll take a roundabout way just to be sure."

"Good," Savid said. "You can also tell Drek that we will send him extra help after dark. In fact, you stay with them instead of coming back here. The rest of us will be along tonight."

Krab acknowledged his instructions and then disappeared into the undergrowth. Savid noted with satisfaction that even the direction of his departure gave no clue to his destination.

"What should we do now?" Ral said.

"We have to wait until dark," Savid said. "In the meantime, we need to know what is happening in Pinchgut. Ral, I know I'm asking a lot, but you know the crunnocks best. Will you and Mot go back there and see what they're up to?"

"No problem," Ral said. "You OK with that?" he asked Mot.

"Maybe we'll get lucky and they'll capture us," Mot said. He had a big grin on his face. "I'd like to have a chat with Sor."

"Never mind your chats," Savid said. "This is all about getting Penney home, not you starting a brawl with the crunnocks."

"I know, but it's nice to dream," Mot said.

"We don't need this to get any more difficult than it already is," Savid said. "Just stay out of sight and let us know what's happening there. Don't take any chances with the crunnocks. If they're up to something, you won't have to look hard to see it."

Assuring her that she had nothing to worry about, Ral and Mot headed off towards Pinchgut. Savid strolled back to where the main group was gathered. She could sense their anxiety and feel their eyes on her as she walked. She stopped and looked at them.

"I know you're uneasy about what's happening," Savid said, "but everything will work out. Each of you should do what I'm going to do—take a nap." With that Savid went to a comfortable spot she had found earlier, under a spruce tree and was soon into one of the deepest sleeps of her long life.

Events in Pinchgut hadn't unfolded as the searchers hoped. There was optimism for a few minutes early in the morning when it appeared that the dogs had found something, but the optimism dwindled as the day wore on. The men plodded through miles of woods, bogs, barrens, and beaches without as much as a trace of the missing girl. They were physically tired, but that wouldn't stop them. It was emotional exhaustion and frustration that threatened the search. They weren't thinking about quitting, but they were beginning to doubt themselves and each other. Ned Duggan could see the uncertainty as the day wore on.

He wasn't part of any of the search lines. Instead, he spent the day travelling throughout the search area, making certain everything was examined, and checking to see if anybody had been lucky enough to find a trace of Penney. He travelled from the mill upriver to the Salmon Hole marsh and then cross-country until he reached the Island Barasway. It was mid-afternoon when he caught up with a dozen men searching through thick woods about halfway between the Island Barasway and Pinchgut.

"How are you fellows doing?" Ned asked.

The searchers broke away from their efforts and gathered around Ned.

"No good news, Ned," one of them said, "but no bad news, either. We haven't seen a thing. Did anybody else have any luck?"

"Not a bit," Ned said. "I don't know what to think. It's like she just vanished."

"Ned, I have to tell you," the same fellow said, "I have my doubts if she's anywhere near here. I can't see how a two-year-old would ever be able to cross this kind of ground."

"I hear you," Ned said. "I'd be lying if I told you I wasn't thinking the same thing myself, but I don't know where else to look. We covered every inch of ground within a couple of miles of her house yesterday and the day before."

"It's the strangest thing I've ever seen," another fellow said. "I'd move heaven and earth to find her, but I can't help thinking that we're not doing any good out here."

Ned knew the search wasn't moving as fast as it should. All day he found the searchers were spending as much time talking as looking.

"I understand," Ned said. "All I can say is that we're here because we've looked everywhere else more than once, and I'm asking you to stick with the search."

"You have no worries about that, sir," the first one said. "We're in this for the long haul. We're not leaving until the little one is back with her parents."

"You'll never know how much I appreciate that, fellows," Ned said. He could see the men in the group agreed with the speaker. "Please God, let something good happen soon, although I don't like the looks of those clouds."

"I don't, either," the searcher said. "We have to find her before the rain starts. Come on fellows, let's get back at it." He led them back to where they were searching before Ned came. "She might be right under our noses. We won't know until we look."

Ned set out again as well, calling more thanks as he departed. He knew at least two men hadn't slowed or hesitated in their efforts. He saw them, but was never able to catch them. One was Michael and the other was Old Joe. Michael had hardly stopped moving since the hour Penney disappeared. Each night, after he tried to comfort Jenny and reassure her that Penney would soon be found, he collapsed on the couch in his kitchen for a few hours of sleep. He was on the move again before dawn. Ned knew he was eating only because Thomas put food in his knapsack. Ned also knew his son would never stop looking until Penney was found or all hope was lost.

Old Joe was something else. He joined the search within ten minutes of Penney going missing, and had covered more ground than men half his age. He spent the first night in the woods, peering by torchlight into every place that could conceal a child. He continued right on through the second day without rest. It was only after he said his few words at the meeting on the second night that he gave in and went home to give his lanky body a few hours sleep. He justified that small concession by reasoning that a short rest would enable him to go longer and harder the next day.

Old Joe made it through life, in an unforgiving time and place, by sizing up situations and taking whatever action was required. He thought he had done a good job of sizing up the search for the little girl. It made sense to him last night to move the search across the river, but now he felt a foreboding, a sense of desperation that he hadn't felt in many years. He travelled about ten miles since first light that morning, not a great distance by his standards, but he had done it through the wettest and most tangled terrain to be found inside the search area. He was never one to take the easy tasks and rely on someone else to do the tough work. Now he was standing on the northern edge of the Salmon Hole marsh about three

150

miles from Pinchgut. He watched as heavy black clouds appeared in the evening sky. They came rushing in from the east like hungry crows gathering over a fresh kill. It was getting dark faster and earlier than it should, and he was chilled by an unseasonable coolness. He was still within hearing range of the mill's steam whistle and its silence told him that no sign of Penney had been found.

"Not good," he thought. "Not good at all."

Far to the east he heard the first rumblings of thunder. He noticed the rumbling was non-stop. A storm was coming, and it was going to be a harsh one. He decided not to take the main trail to Pinchgut. Instead, he would follow the river downstream to the mill. It would take him a couple of hours longer, and it would be after dark before he got home, but he would be covering extra ground, which just might be the place that held the little girl. Every instinct of his long life told him that, if she was going to be found alive, she had to be found today. The gathering storm was ominous; it was going to be more than the usual summer thunder squall and it seemed to harbour ill will for anything in its path. The coming storm, the failure of the search, and the responsibility he felt for moving the search across the river, resurrected the unaccustomed feelings of doubt and despair. He was not given to accepting failure easily, and as he set out towards the river, he began to go over the events of the last three days. What did they miss? There must be something.

Chapter 10 - The Storm

Darkness and rain fell on Pinchgut at the same time. Most of the searchers were still a considerable distance from the community when they finally had to concede that conditions were too bad to continue the search. In groups of two and three they left the woods and marshes and made their way back to the schoolhouse. They were a sorry looking lot—every one of them exhausted, soaked to the skin, and almost blue with the cold. It was plain to see that they were driving their bodies to the limit and giving the search everything they had. This evening, though, for the first time, uncertainty could be seen in their eyes. Until now, they knew the prospects were good for finding the child alive. The weather had been warm. Hunger or thirst wouldn't kill her in a few days, and as long as she hadn't been hurt, there was every reason to believe she was alive. Now, however, the prospects were worsening by the minute.

The men accepted bowls of hot soup and cups of steaming tea from the women waiting at the school. All of them had to answer the same questions. "Did you see anything? Any sign at all?" They shook their heads and gave the same answer—nothing. They gathered at the long wooden tables and talked among themselves while they gulped their food.

"A grown man couldn't stay out in this squall, never mind a little child."

"It's not good."

"Maybe it won't last long. Tomorrow might be hot."

"Soup's good."

"Where else can we look?"

"Is there any point in going out again tonight?"

"Can't see anything."

"We have to figure out something."

"She's out there somewhere."

"Pass the butter."

Meanwhile, a short distance up the river above Pinchgut, Sor stood in front of the crunnocks.

"Are you ready?" he yelled.

The assembly of scoundrels roared and waved their clubs.

"Are we going to put an end to the starrigans?"

More shouts of approval.

"It's cold and wet now, but it's going to get a lot hotter if the starrigans have the guts to show up. Remember: when we get them on the island not one of them gets off. Right?"

The clan roared again. Sor was well pleased. They were pumped and ready to go. He was looking forward to the fight with the starrigans. They had made him look bad too often in the last couple of days. He was especially hoping he could get his hands on that traitorous leech, Ral. He planned to make an example of him that every single crunnock would remember for a long time. Teaming up with the starrigans wouldn't look so attractive to any of the rest of them after tonight.

"Let's go!" Sor yelled. The clan hollered in support. "It's time to get rid of the starrigans." Sor led them through the woods towards the island, and to what he expected to be one of the most momentous nights in crunnock history.

Mot watched them leave. He had spent most of the afternoon hiding within listening distance of Sor. Every time the crunnock leader moved along the riverbank, Mot moved with him, always staying out of sight in the undergrowth, almost under the crunnock's nose. Now that he knew where the crunnocks were going, he headed back to the other side of the river to rendezvous with Ral who had stayed near the schoolhouse to keep an eye on the people. The trip across the bridge was uneventful and he found Ral right away.

"What's happening here?" Mot asked.

"Not much," Ral said. "Most of the searchers are back and they look pretty gloomy. What's Sor up to?"

"Him and the rest of the scoundrels just left for the second island," Mot said. "He has to be the biggest idiot I ever saw."

"He's all right when you don't know the difference," Ral said. "But after you meet someone like Savid, it's not easy to put up with Sor."

"Speaking of Savid," Mot said, "we should be getting back to her. There's not much happening here and we know what the crunnocks are up to."

"Let's go," Ral said.

As darkness fell, Savid decided it would be safe for the clan to leave the woods on the side of Island Pond and go to where they were keeping Penney. The starrigans were elated. Most of them would be seeing the little girl for the first time since she was taken from home. Savid had carefully guarded the child's location, revealing it only to the caregivers and messengers. Leaving Gable to wait for Mot and Ral, Savid led the rest of the clan around Island Pond and along the side of the river. Krab spotted them coming and went to meet them. He led them to the secluded little grove where they were hiding Penney.

Seeing the little girl was a moment filled with emotion for many of the starrigans. They knew the details of her capture and rescue, but it was only when they came face to face with her that they grasped the enormity of the quest. Starrigans knew humans as creatures that shaped the world around them. Yet, here was this tiny creature, albeit much bigger than any starrigan, who couldn't live without constant care. It seemed as if the clan suddenly came to the sobering realization that this was not a game. This little girl was in serious trouble and was going to die if they couldn't get her home soon.

Soc was overwhelmed by the poignancy of the moment. Since the hour that they took Penney away from the crunnocks, the soft-hearted starrigan stayed within touching distance of the child. Now, with the appearance of the rest of her clan, she knew her time with Penney was drawing to an end. She was only too aware that there was no way to be certain that the conclusion would be the happy one they wanted. She was sobbing softly when Savid came to her. The old starrigan lifted Soc's chin and looked into her eyes.

"You have done well, my little one," Savid said. "Penney needed to trust us and to know that we are her friends. You earned that trust for us and because of it we are able to help her." She wiped away the tears streaming down over Soc's face. "Always remember the strength of kindness; it can remove barriers that the strongest warriors can't penetrate. It is the embodiment of friendship."

"I will," Soc said.

"It isn't always easy to be kind," Savid said, "but it is always right. There are many in the world around us who don't understand that yet, and see kindness as a form of weakness. They will only come to understand the real meaning of strength by watching creatures like you doing things they can't. I'm very proud of you."

"What's going to happen now?" Soc asked. "Are we going to take her home?"

"I hope so," Savid said. "It depends on what news Ral and Mot have for us. Right now, though, I want to move her as close to the trail to home as we can."

"I can do that," Soc said. She walked over to Penney, who was surrounded by curious starrigans. Savid accompanied her.

"It's going to be a miserable night," Savid said. "I don't want to try to lead her through the woods or across marshes. If it's safe, we'll use the trail to take her home."

Soc had only to tug at Penney's dress to get the child to follow her. All of the other starrigans were fascinated by the bond between them. Penney enjoyed the company of all the starrigans, but it was obvious that Soc was the one she trusted without reservation. She toddled along behind Soc, with the rest of the starrigans following on the ground and in the trees close by. As they moved, they were aware of the roll of thunder and flashes of lightning in the distance.

"It's going to be pretty nasty when that reaches here," Krab said to Savid.

"It is for sure," Savid said.

The storm descended on Pinchgut like a mighty hammer falling on an anvil. It parked squarely over the little hamlet and moved no farther. The roar of the wind across the rooftops and down the chimneys was unlike anything the people had ever heard before. It drove the rain in great sheets that not only added to the din, making it necessary to shout to be heard, but also took away the ability to see anything more than a few feet from one's face. The deluge soaked everything not under cover within minutes, but still it wasn't the wind and rain that alarmed the people. Their attention was seized by the frenzy of the thunder and lightning. The lightning took command of the night away from the darkness. There was so little time between flashes that it appeared as though the blinding light was constant and the brief instances of darkness were intermittent. Meanwhile thunder shook the world. Every clap was right overhead and the ground underfoot trembled like it was receiving the recoil of a thousand cannons.

Old Joe was out in the middle of it all. He had made his way along the riverbank from the Salmon Hole marsh and was upriver past the Crow's Nest when the full fury of the storm fell on him.

"Good thing I don't leak," was the only consideration he gave to the weather. The only significant thing about the storm, as far as he was concerned, was that Penney was out in it. He was moving slower than he moved all day because of the low visibility and the slippery rocks underfoot. He could see little as he left the Crow's Nest and made his way downstream to Cat House Island. He knew the little island well and studied it carefully as the lightning illuminated it as bright as day. He peered among the few big trees growing, out of reach of ice, in the centre of the island. He saw nothing that interested him and continued downriver with a heavy heart. Just past the second island the sight of something moving towards him along the riverbank interrupted his thoughts.

"What the devil is that?" he asked out loud, as he tried to see through the rain in the flashes of lightning.

Sor was leading the mob of crunnocks along the river-bank towards the second island. Moving about in the horrible weather was as difficult for them as it was for the people. They had just about reached the island when a human voice sounded, almost in their midst. They looked up to see a man, illuminated by the light-ning,  standing in their path.

"Everybody in the woods," Sor yelled.

The mob moved as one into the nearby trees and stopped when they were out of sight. They looked back towards the man. He was peering through the rain trying to see where they had gone. He looked into the woods, up and down the riverbank, and out across the river. It was obvious to the crunnocks that he didn't know where they were, but it quickly became apparent he had seen them.

"Where are you?" Joe yelled. "Come out so I can see you. I don't know what you are but you don't belong here. Now get out here and let me see you."

Old Joe thought for a second he had come upon some wildlife, but he discounted it immediately.

"Rabbits don't move in herds and ducks don't walk when they want to go somewhere," he thought. "No animal in their right mind would be out in this storm anyway."

No, whatever he saw didn't belong to the woods around Pinchgut, but he had no doubt it had something to do with the missing child. Most men would be terrified to face such an unknown entity, but Old Joe gave up being afraid long ago. Fear, he reasoned, was only for those with something to lose. He owned nothing of value and he had already lived more than his share of years, so not even the prospect of losing his life concerned him. Now he was furious and roared above the howl of the storm.

"Get back here and let me see you, whatever the hell you are. What are you afraid of? I'm by myself. Or do you only pick on little girls?" He paced back and forth along the riverbank. "Show your faces you bloody cowards. I knew there was more to this than a child wandering off by herself. No wonder we can't find her. The fairies got her."

Sor and the crunnocks cowered behind the trees.

"He's a madman," Drog said to Sor.

"Shut up," Sor said.

Old Joe stood there, seething and waiting for a response in the middle of the tempest, but none came.

"Listen to me whatever you are," he shouted above the storm. "Either the young one shows up tonight or I promise, starting tomorrow, I'll rid this land of you if I have to burn every tree and bush in the place to do it."

Seeing that he was getting no reply he finally set out again towards home, but his mind was refocused. Now he knew why they couldn't find the child. He didn't know what the solution was yet, but he understood something else was at work here.

"The fairies have her," he said. "Well, they're not keeping her, not if I can help it. How the hell do we get something back from them anyway?" His mind was racing as he bulled his way through the storm to home.

The unexpected meeting with Old Joe left Sor shaken. He knew he should have anticipated that some of the searchers might still be out in spite of the weather. Instead, he let his guard down and allowed the man to walk right in among them. There was no doubt he saw them and identified them for what they were. Worse still, he also connected them with the missing child and vowed to take action if the child wasn't returned. Sor knew from the old tales of his clan that the humans were capable of going to great lengths to get rid of his kind, and it was a battle Sor didn't want to fight.

"What a mess," he thought. He waited for a few more minutes to make certain the crazed man was gone and then led the crunnocks back out to the riverbank. Moments later they jumped across some rocks and were out on the island. Once there, he gathered his clan around him.

"This is the place," Sor said. "Let's see if they have the guts to show up. Be ready in case they try to surprise us."

"Sor, how long are we going to wait in this rain?" asked Drog.

"You got other plans for tonight?" Sor asked. "We'll stay until daylight if we have to. They won't be able to say they were here and we weren't. Keep your eyes open for them."

The second island was a low-lying bit of gravel in the middle of the river, rising only a few inches above the level of the water. The spring floods and coarse sandy soil prevented anything other than tough sinewy grasses and bulrushes from growing on it. The crunnocks huddled in the middle of the island, trying to protect themselves from the fury of the storm while they waited for the starrigans.

Meanwhile, miles upstream, the downpour filled the headwaters of the river to overflowing. Water poured into the Back River from Big Pond and Bad Pond. The northern and eastern tributaries were flooded beyond capacity. All of the water emptied into the main river creating a torrent of epic proportions that was roaring towards Pinchgut.

Jenny was hysterical. All evening she watched as the searchers returned empty-handed. She saw the storm get closer and closer, and when its fury descended she could no longer contain her anguish. Her plaintive wails escaped through the walls of the little house.

"My baby! My baby! She can't live in this. I'll never see her again. Oh please God, help us."

The distraught mother could not be consoled. Michael was still out searching and Jenny ignored the reassurances offered by the other women. Not even Ned, her father-in-law, whom she adored, could comfort her. Since Penney went missing, he dropped in every time he had a chance. He always remained optimistic, pointing out how the weather was warm, the great number of men searching, and saying no news was good news. He never let Jenny have any doubt about Penney's safe return. It was different today. Perhaps it was his haggard appearance or maybe, for the first time, she saw the worry in his eyes, but he was unable to convince her that there was still hope. No matter what he said, she shook her head and cried harder.

"She's gone. I know it. I'll never see her again. My baby's gone." Finally Jenny sought the solitude of her bedroom. Her pitiful cries coming down the stairs broke the hearts of everyone in the house, but none of them could provide any solace.

Father Quigley was in the schoolhouse when he learned of Jenny's breakdown. He made his way through the darkness and raging storm to her home. He noticed, as soon as he entered the house, that the mood was the same as a funeral.

"She's upstairs in her room, Father," Ned said. "She's having a bad time."

The priest went up the stairs and knocked on the door. Getting no response, other than the sobs from within, he opened the door and went inside. The single kerosene lamp did little to illuminate the room. Nevertheless, he was shocked by the sight that greeted him. Jenny had changed out of her everyday clothes and was wearing a black mourning dress. She was lying face down on the bed. The priest was unsure of what to do or say, so he just sat on the edge of the bed and placed his hand on her shoulder. She turned over and her eyes met his.

"Why, Father? I don't understand why I couldn't keep her. Why was she taken away?"

"I don't know, my child," Father Quigley said. "Some things were never meant for us to understand." This was not the time to try and explain that God has a reason for everything. He was surprised, however, at her next words.

"Father, can you have a funeral Mass for her?"

He thought for a moment and chose his words carefully.

"Of course I'll have a Mass if that's what you want. But I won't have a funeral Mass. Jenny, I know how bad everything seems right now and I'm not going to lie to you. Maybe we won't see Penney alive again, but we don't know that." He paused to pick his words. "If she is still alive then we must not fail her. If she's out there hanging on, we can't give up. Do you understand me?"

Jenny nodded. The priest noticed her sobs had abated a little and he knew that somehow he had found the right words.

"We will have a Mass, but it's going to be a Mass asking for help, not a funeral. OK?"

Jenny nodded.

"I'm going up to the school to get the place ready. When Michael gets home and you're both ready, come up to the school and I'll say the Mass. All right?"

She nodded again and tried to dry away some of the tears.

"That's better," he said. "I'll send Sues up to help you. We'll all get through this together. I promise you."

He was pleased that he had been able to settle Jenny down, but as he went back out into the tempest he couldn't help but think he may have done nothing except postpone the inevitable.

164

Savid and the starrigans were facing another problem. The thunder and lightning terrified Penney and she was refusing to move. Making matters worse, she was soaked to the skin and the temperature had fallen to an unseasonable low. They were gathered in the lee of a huge spruce tree that had blown down in a previous storm. The windfall provided some protection from the wind and rain, but didn't shelter them from the thunder and lightning or the mind-numbing cold. Most of the starrigans gathered around Penney to try and give her some warmth. Savid huddled with Krab, Soc, Drek and some others trying to figure out what to do. As they talked Gable, Ral, and Mot arrived. Savid's relief was evident when Mot assured her the crunnocks had gone to the island.

"Excellent," she said. "This is the opportunity we have been waiting for. The crunnocks are out of the way, so now we have to get Penney home before something else goes wrong."

"How are we going to manage that?" Krab asked. "Even if we could get her to move, she would never make it home through this storm. She'll perish on the trail."

"She'll perish here if we don't do something," Mot said.

"If we can't get her to go to them maybe we can get them to come to her," Gable said.

"What do you mean?" Krab asked.

"I'm not sure," Gable said. "But we have to get her in touch with her people. We have to find a way to get them to come here."

Soc noticed Ral standing at the back of the group, looking very sombre. This was the first time that she had seen him since Mot had taken him prisoner. The sensitive starrigan noticed right away that he no longer looked like the tough warrior he was a couple of days earlier. She walked over to him.

"The others told me how you saved Gable from the dog," she said. "You're very brave."

"I don't feel so brave now," he said. "I would sooner face that hunting dog another hundred times than look at the child once. I've been dreading this moment."

"You didn't know things would be this bad when you took her," Soc said. "You're not bad. You just didn't know the difference."

"Look at her," he said. "She's cold and frightened. She was happy and safe before we took her. Now, because of me, she's out in the woods in the middle of a storm."

"Ral, that's your name, isn't it?"

He nodded.

"They call me Soc."

"I heard about you. You're the one who has been looking after her, aren't you?"

"Yes," she said, "but I want to talk about you. We know what you did was wrong, but it could be worse."

"How could it possibly be worse?"

"Well," Soc said, "what kind of predicament would we be in if the crunnocks still had Gable? What would we be able to do if we didn't know they were up on the island together?" She took Ral's hand. "Others might not have helped. You did and it made a difference."

"Thank you," Ral said. "I wish I could find a way to get her home. She doesn't even have a cap to keep the rain off her head because of me . . ." His voice trailed off as an idea began to take shape in his head. Then his face lit up. "Her cap! That's it!" He ran to where Savid and the others were talking.

"Mot, come here. I know how to get this done. I have an idea that will bring the people right to her." Ral proceeded to lay out a plan, and they all agreed it was worth trying.

Old Joe made it home just in time to meet Lucy getting ready to go out the door. His wife was shocked by his dishevelled appearance and pulled him into the kitchen.

"Thank God you're alive," she said. "But look at the state you're in. Get those wet clothes off. I'll get some dry clothes for you to put on, and then I'll make you a cup of tea."

"I'm all right, woman," Old Joe said. "I don't want any tea. The fairies got that child. That's why we can't find her."

"Don't be talking foolishness, Joe," Lucy said. "If anybody else hears you saying something like that, they'll think the fairies got you. Now, put those dry clothes on while I boil the kettle."

"She's right," the old man thought as he changed his clothes. "Nobody will believe me if I tell them what I saw. They'll only say, 'Old Joe's finally gone daft.' I better figure this out before I say anything else." He turned to Lucy. "I think I will have a mug of tea. Where are you going?"

"Father Quigley is saying Mass up in the school," Lucy said. "Are you going to come up?"

"You go ahead," Joe said. "I'll come along as soon as I finish my tea and rest a bit."

Joe sat on the couch by the stove while she poured his tea and laid out some bread and cold cuts. After he indicated to her that the food was sufficient and assured her that he would be all right, she wrapped herself in an oilskin coat and went out into the storm. He knew she was as tough as he was. He held the firm opinion that he never would have made it through life without her. Why then, he pondered, had both of them been allowed to live long lives in hard times while a little girl, who was so loved and cared for, was taken away?

"Because there's more to this than meets the eye, that's why," he said out loud, his anger rising again. He shoved the tea mug away and got back on his feet. He pulled on his heavy oilskin coat once again and went out. The storm had gotten worse during the short time that he was inside. Outdoors again, his eyes needed a moment to grow accustomed to the dark.

"It's blacker than the inside of a tar bucket," he said. As his eyes adjusted to the darkness, he noticed something just outside his fence. "What's that?" he said, moving towards it.

Many of the searchers assembled in the schoolhouse on the hill knew Old Joe had been travelling alone most of the day, and were concerned about his well-being. They were relieved to hear from Lucy that he was safely home. Michael and Jenny arrived soon after Lucy. The crowd began to put away the food and rearrange the furniture, transforming the search headquarters into a church for Father Quigley to say Mass. The priest, for his part, was pleased to see that, although Jenny was still distraught, she had changed out of the mourning clothes she wore earlier and was now wearing her everyday clothing.

The young couple sat together by the wall waiting for the Mass to begin. Individually, and in clusters of two and three, their friends and neighbours took a moment to speak with them. Most found the moment awkward and the right words were hard to come by. Michael kept his arm around Jenny while she sat there sobbing. He did all of the talking, thanking each one for their support and acknowledging the tremendous effort that his friends and neighbours were making to find Penney. Ned stood nearby as well, reiterating the family's gratitude.

Father Quigley came over and spoke to them. He was wearing his clerical vestments and asked if it was OK to begin the Mass. Michael nodded and then led Jenny to seats in the front row.

The priest began, "In the name of the Father . . ."

Just a little over a mile from where the people of Pinchgut were assembled in the schoolhouse, one of the crunnocks pushed his way through the cronies gathered around Sor.

"Sor," the crunnock cried. "The water is up over the rocks. There's no way any of the starrigans are going to get out here tonight. Come and look at it for yourself."

Sor followed his anxious subordinate towards the edge of the island. He could see right away that the island was a lot smaller now than it was when the clan arrived earlier. The stepping stones they used had disappeared under the torrent of water. The crunnocks ran to every side of the little island only to find more than half of it was now under water. As each flash of lightning lit up the river valley, they peered through the driving rain in an effort to find some way off the island, but there was no escape. They were trapped and the river was rising.

"What are we going to do?"

"We're going to get wet, you fools," Sor said. "I'm going to do away with that hag of a starrigan when I get my hands on her!"

As the Mass in the schoolhouse progressed, and the water in the river continued to rise, the fury of the storm grew to a terrifying intensity. The flashes of lightning followed each other so closely, that they made it possible to see the length and breadth of Pinchgut almost as easily as in the midday sun. Every clap of thunder crashing down on the little schoolhouse shook the floor and rattled the kerosene lamps mounted on the wall. The howl from the wind racing across the roof and down the chimney sounded like the screams of the damned to the faithful praying inside. Father Quigley tried hard to keep his congregation focussed on the Mass, but it was impossible to ignore the storm that was shaking the building.

On the island up in the river terror seized the crunnocks as the water continued to rise. They were soon forced into one cluster, while the torrent raged around them. Some of them were forced to stand in the rising water as the edges of the island continued to be submerged. The bravado they had displayed a few hours earlier was gone, and they pushed and shoved each other in an effort to stay out of the river. It was a futile effort. One, who had been forced to the outside of the group, lost his footing and was seized by the floodwaters. His screams were lost in the noise of the storm. Soon another and then another were washed away in the cascade.

The raging waters raced downriver and through Pinchgut. The wall of water broke the boom in front of the mill allowing the thousands of logs to escape to the open bay. Some of the crunnocks washing down the river managed to grab onto the logs, while others swam for hours looking for dry land. Sor was one of the last to be washed away. He passed under the bridge and out of Pinchgut as the storm reached the peak of its fury, still screaming his anger at the old starrigan whom he blamed for all of his misfortunes.

Father Quigley ended the Mass as soon as he could. The fear that his parishoners was experiencing was evident, and he knew that in spite of their piety this was not a time to expect them to stay quiet. After the final blessing they huddled together in small groups, looking at the walls and ceilings, as every crash of thunder threatened to bring the building down around them. In the schoolyard a spruce tree, forty feet tall and more than a century old, received a direct lightning hit and exploded as though it was bursting from the depths of hell. The likes of it had never been witnessed before. Jenny's fragile composure was shattered. Ned looked out the window as the lightning lit up the river, just in time to see the boom holding the logs give way and all of the logs go racing towards the salt water. Instinctively, he knew that many of the men would have to be taken off the search to spend the next several days recovering the logs. There was no choice. The economic survival of the entire place depended upon turning those logs into lumber, and when the boom burst a full year's income escaped.

"What else can go wrong?" he thought.

"Ahaaiiieee! Ahaaiiieee! There's something out there!" One of the women was screaming and staggering backwards, trying to get away from a window on the other side of the room. Her arms were stretched out in front of her as though she was trying to push back something before it could grab her. Her eyes were fixed open—locked on something terrifying.

The men rushed to the windows. The flashes of lightning illuminated an apparition unlike anything they had seen before. A huge dark hulk, bent and top-heavy, was staggering across the yard towards the school door. Women screamed and the men turned towards each other in alarm as heavy footsteps were heard in the outside porch. Then the door

crashed open and the spectre fell into their midst. It lurched across the room and fell to its knees before collapsing face down on the floor.

"My God, it's Old Joe!"

Lucy was the first to reach her husband. She tried to turn him over, but couldn't budge the old giant. Ned and Father Quigley grabbed hold of him and turned him on his back. As they did, he let go of the bundle he was carrying. It was wrapped in his great black oilskin coat, and when he rolled on his back the coat fell open. Pandemonium erupted.

Wrapped securely inside was the missing child.

Jenny flung herself through the crowd and grabbed her daughter.

"Thank God! Oh thank God! I have you back! Mike, we have her back. She's alive. She's alive." Jenny laughed and sobbed all at once. Michael clutched them both in his arms and, for the first time since the ordeal began, broke down completely. He buried his face on his wife's shoulder and wept uncontrollably.

Everybody wanted to see Penney. The crowd surged around the ecstatic family. Questions came from all sides.

"Is it really her?"

"Is she OK?"

"Is she hurt?"

"Does she look all right?"

"Where was she? Joe, where did you find her?"

Ned Duggan was the first to notice that Old Joe was still lying on the floor and Lucy was lying across his chest, crying.

"Oh no," Ned said. "Father Quigley! Father Quigley!"

The priest rushed to Joe's side and began to administer the last rites, but it was too late. It was plain for all to see that the old man's long life was finally over. The crowd was stunned. From terror to jubilation, to shock and sorrow, in just a few moments. It was more than most of them could cope with, and the sounds of weeping spread through the room. Jenny, still clutching Penney tightly, knelt alongside Lucy. Long minutes passed before she could say anything.

"I'm so sorry. I don't know what to say. We didn't even get to thank him. He found her and brought her back to us and we didn't get a chance to say thank you."

Lucy smiled through her tears and then leaned over and kissed the little girl. "He did find her, didn't he? That's all he wanted to do." She wiped a tear from her face. "He's happy. I know he is."

Jenny nodded and then asked the question that was on everybody's mind. "How did he do it? Where was she? Look, she's covered in bakeapple juice."

"Are you OK?" Lucy asked the child.

Penney smiled and nodded.

"Who took care of you?" Jenny asked.

"Little people," she whispered to her mom.

Chapter 11 - A Bright New Day

The river was still a swollen torrent the next afternoon. The starrigans could only gaze across it towards their home in Little Brook Bottom. It would be at least another full day before they could cross, but they didn't mind at all. The sun was bright and hot, and the air smelled fresh and clean after the thunderstorm. They had much to talk about.

One of their subjects of conversation was, at that moment, lying at the high-water mark on a rocky piece of beach several miles from Pinchgut. Sor was bedraggled and beaten. He had swum for hours through the night trying to make his way to land. Now, surrounded by flotsam and sea-weed, he was an uninspiring sight for sure. He could see several of his clan making their way along the beach towards him. One of them was Lirap. He stood up to meet them, but their words gave him no comfort.

"Looks like we really showed the starrigans something," Lirap said.

"Yeah, thanks a lot, Sor," added another. "What have you got in mind next?"

"Where are all the others?" Sor asked.

"Strung out for miles all along the shore," Lirap said. "It will take days to find everybody. We're lucky most of us weren't killed." He stood face to face with Sor. "Get it through your head right now, Sor: that's the last time we'll be following you anywhere. You haven't got a clue about what you're doing."

Sor was flabbergasted by the newfound audacity of the crunnock, but it was obvious by the expressions of the others that they felt the same way. His days as their leader appeared to be over. The crunnocks continued up the beach without him.

"That old starrigan hasn't seen the last of me. As sure as there are trees in the woods, I will find her and bring her down," he said.

Things were still not back to normal in Pinchgut, but at least the people were dealing with matters that they understood. Most of the men were busy retrieving the thousands of logs that escaped when the boom burst. They were scattered all around the bay and along the shoreline. It would take the mill workers the better part of a week to gather them together and get them back in front of the mill where they belonged. They had to be collected in smaller booms and then towed back when the wind and tides were favourable. It was backbreaking and tedious work, but the Pinchgut men were receiving some much-needed help from the men who had come to take part in the search and were now staying for Old Joe's funeral.

Old Joe had been a larger-than-life figure when he was alive. In death, he was fast becoming a legend. He was one of the "old hands" who used his wits and his strength to overcome every challenge and obstacle life threw at him. Now washed, shaved, and dressed in the best clothes that he owned, he lay in a coffin resting on four chairs in the front room of his house. Ned and Thomas spent the previous night making the coffin from the finest lumber the mill produced and, early in the morning, helped to lay him in it. Lucy wore a black dress and the window shades were drawn shut to signify the house was in mourning, but apart from those prerequisite symbols, there was little sign of sorrow.

The house was alive with chatter as those gathered to pay their respects regaled each other with tales of Old Joe's exploits. There were, as expected, stories of his great physical strength. No log was too big to carry, no horse too wild to put shoes on, no trail too long to walk. Joe was also held in high regard for his ingenuity. He had outwitted the slyest foxes and repaired everything from broken fingers to the main engine in the mill. Everybody had a story to tell which contributed to the greatness of the man, but it was when the tales of his kindness started to come out that even those closest to him were amazed. It was something he kept well hidden under a tough crust.

It seemed as if every family that ever had a difficult time had been on the receiving end of assistance from Old Joe. All through the day and into the evening stories were told. It became obvious that, beyond what was needed to provide sustenance for himself and Lucy, Joe had given away just about everything that passed through his hands. "No wonder we didn't have anything," Lucy said. "He gave it all away."

In the evening Jenny and Michael came with Penney to pay their respects. The little girl was still too young to understand what was happening, but in the years ahead Jenny would make sure she understood the goodness of the man who brought her home. Michael and his family promised Lucy that she would never want for anything as long as she lived. It was a promise Ned Duggan intended to make sure was kept.

Michael and Jenny were still unable to provide any answers to the question on everybody's mind—where was Penney and how did Joe find her? She didn't say anything to explain her absence beyond the single reference she made about little people. Her parents explained that she appeared to have been looked after somehow since she wasn't hungry and there wasn't as much as a fly-bite on her body. It was only because her dress was covered in bakeapple juice that they knew she had spent time outdoors. It was a mystery they would never solve.

The only creatures who did know the whole story were sitting and lying along the banks of the river, not far from the ridge where Krab had first encountered Michael more than two years earlier. They had watched the sun go down and now countless stars penetrated the black velvet of the night sky. It was a moonless night, which served to make the brilliance of the stars infinitely greater. The clan was chatting idly while they waited for Krab and Gable to return from Pinchgut. Both of them soon appeared.

"She's too young to explain anything," Gable said, "and the old man didn't say a word before he died."

"That's good," Savid said. "It's sad that such a good man died, but it's better they know nothing about us—or the crunnocks, for that matter."

"Do you think he knew about us?" Krab asked.

"He knew something," Ral said. "When Mot and I saw him coming out of his house, we pulled Penney's apron up where he could see it. He came after it right away, just like Jenny went after her cap when we threw it in the river, but he knew it wasn't the wind blowing it."

"That's right," Mot said. "He talked to us just like he could see us under the apron. He said it was a good thing we came to take him to Penney because he would have made it bad for us if we hadn't. I don't know how he knew but he sure seemed to know we had her."

"Maybe he was just guessing," said Soc.

"No, he knew," Ral said. "He even tested us, didn't he, Mot?"

"That's right," Mot said. "When we were coming across the marsh, just before we got to where all of you were, he said he was tired and yelled out for us to stop. We kept going so he would think the wind was blowing the apron, but he just stopped and sat down."

"He said he wasn't going to chase the wind and if we didn't wait he was going to turn around and go home," Ral said.

"What did you do?" Krab asked.

"What could we do? We had to wait for him," Ral said. "When he was ready he stood up and said, 'OK, let's go.' So we just went to where you were with Penney and he followed us."

"Do you think he saw any of us there?" Soc said.

"I doubt it," Mot said. "Soc, you were the last one to leave Penney, weren't you? When did you leave?"

"When I saw the apron coming," Soc said. "I'm sure he didn't see me, though. I wiggled out through the back of the lean-to we built. As soon as Penney started to cry for me, he found her."

"Did he say anything?" Savid asked.

"Yes," Soc said. "He kept hugging Penney and telling her he was going to take her home to her mommy and daddy. He noticed the lean-to, and said something about it being pretty handy work for a two-year-old. Then he tucked Penney inside his coat and carried her back to Pinchgut."

"Did you see anything else, Ral?" Savid asked.

"No," Ral said. "Mot and I stayed with him until he got back to the school. It was unbelievable how hard he had to work. He couldn't see very well in the storm and there was nothing leading him. He fell into a dozen bog holes."

"He didn't let go of Penney until he was inside the school," Mot said. "It was really hard going and I knew he was tired, but I didn't expect him to die."

"The old man died and the child lives," Savid said. She walked to the water's edge and stared out over the river into the darkness. She was smiling when she turned to face her clan. "I suspect he had a greater understanding of what was happening than we realize. Don't be sad for him. He would never want it, and it's not necessary."

"What do we do now?" Krab asked. "Do you think we will see the crunnocks again very soon?"

"Maybe, maybe not. Perhaps it will be a good thing if we do," Savid said, smiling at Ral. "There's good in all things if we take the time to look for it. In the meantime, I suggest we get on with enjoying our lives. It's something we'll only get one chance to do right."

The End

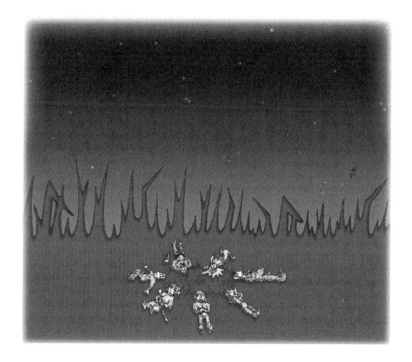

Acknowledgements

Thanks to Mom for always encouraging me to read and write.

To family on all sides for their support along the way; especially to Amanda who was the first person to read every word.

To Joe Byrne, for assuring me I was doing something worth seeing through.

To Anne Marie Hagan and Joe Ryan for their nudges in the right direction.

To Ed Kavanaugh for his merciless editing and professional guidance.

To Donna Francis and Angela Pitcher at Creative Book Publishing for bringing it all together.

To Dana Carter for patiently turning my words into pictures.

To Len for "technical" advice.

Above all, I want to thank you, the reader. The greatest tale a writer conjures up means nothing unless someone reads it.

Harold Davis